STEVE BARLOW AND

Vernon Bright and

Illustrated by
GEO PARKIN

PUFFIN BOOKS

PUFFIN BOOKS

Published by the Penguin Group
Penguin Books Ltd, 80 Strand, London WC2R 0RL, England
Penguin Putnam Inc., 375 Hudson Street, New York, New York 10014, USA
Penguin Books Australia Ltd, Ringwood, Victoria, Australia
Penguin Books Canada Ltd, 10 Alcorn Avenue, Toronto, Ontario, Canada M4V 3B2
Penguin Books India (P) Ltd, 11 Community Centre, Panchsheel Park, New Delhi – 110 017, India
Penguin Books (NZ) Ltd, Cnr Rosedale and Airborne Roads, Albany, Auckland, New Zealand
Penguin Books (South Africa) (Pty) Ltd, 24 Sturdee Avenue, Rosebank 2196 South Africa

Penguin Books Ltd, Registered Offices: 80 Strand, London WC2R 0RL, England

www.penguin.com

First published 2001
2

Text copyright © Steve Barlow and Steve Skidmore, 2001
Illustrations copyright © Geo Parkin, 2001
All rights reserved

Set in 12½/18 Palatino

Made and printed in England by Clays Ltd, St Ives plc

British Library Cataloguing in Publication Data
A CIP catalogue record for this book is available from the British Library

ISBN 0–141–30586–X

CONTENTS

The two Steves would like to thank Trevor Day for his invaluable advice on the scientific principles referred to in this book, and for pointing out which of our ideas were 'come on, boys, that's totally impossible' and which were merely 'completely gaga, but what the heck, it's sci-fi.' Any remaining inaccuracies are what we managed to slip in while he was looking the other way.

Readers should note that moving faster than the speed of light is not allowed – especially in the school corridors, shopping centres and around the sides of swimming pools.

Offenders will be dealt with severely by the authorities – if they can catch them.

CHAPTER ONE

Bright's Big Bang

John Watt eyed the Big Red Button nervously. 'What does it do?' he asked.

Vernon Bright raised a mysterious finger. 'Aha,' he said.

John gave Bright a worried look. It wasn't exactly that he didn't trust him. Bright was very reliable – unfortunately. He could be relied on to cause chaos, mayhem and panic wherever he went, particularly when he had *that* look in his eyes, and said things like 'aha'.

Bright kept his eyes on the stage and gave a secretive smile that worried John even more.

They were sitting in the lighting control room

1

at the back of the school hall. Below them, an audience of mums, dads and rebellious brothers and sisters watched with glazed expressions as the school orchestra scraped and tooted its way through what was allegedly a performance of Tchaikovsky's *1812 Overture*. At the front of the stage, Ms Willis, the Head of Music, was waving her arms about as if she were conducting the London Symphony Orchestra.

The control room was soundproofed. The bangs and squawks of the players echoed tinnily from a loudspeaker above Bright's head. He reached for the volume control and turned it down.

'What a racket! What's it supposed to be about anyway?' asked Bright as the sweating musicians negotiated their fitful way through the score.

Bright had no time for any pursuit that wasn't scientific. His knowledge of music was nil. John's wasn't much better, but he at least recognized the *1812* from music lessons with Ms Willis, who had explained the story behind the piece in great detail.

'The *1812 Overture*? It's supposed to be about Napoleon's retreat from Moscow,' John told him helpfully. 'The French army captured the city, but the Russians had all packed up and gone and there was no food, so the French soldiers ended up eating horses and their own boots, and then winter came and they had to retreat, and the Russians gave them a good kicking and got Moscow back.'

'When did that happen?'

John stared at him. 'Eighteen twelve,' he said carefully. 'That's why it's called the *1812 Overture*.'

'Oh,' said Bright carelessly. 'I thought eighteen twelve meant nearly quarter-past six.'

John rolled his eyes. 'The bit you can hear now is supposed to represent the French Army,' he said.

Bright listened for a moment and shook his head. 'Sounds like a cat being strangled in a bottling plant,' he said happily.

John groaned inwardly. Bright was in a good mood, and when Bright was in a good mood it was a pound to a mouldy peanut that somebody was going to suffer. Usually that somebody was John. He shot another nervous glance at the Big Red Button.

Having volunteered to help Bright (or rather,

having been volunteered by Bright to help him) do the lighting for the school concert, John was familiar with most of the equipment in the control room: the lighting board, the sound mixing desk and various bits of gadgetry. But he had never before seen the box that sat next to the sound desk. It featured a key sticking into a lock, an LED display, a row of switches, and what John had immediately christened the Big Red Button. There was nothing shy and retiring about this button. It looked the sort of button that would be used to launch a space shuttle, or World War Three.

John gazed at it and bit his fingers. 'What does it do?' he asked again.

'Aha!'

'Could you be a bit more specific?' John put aside the science-fiction magazine he had been trying to read in the dim light. 'You know what Ms Willis said about the lighting. You know she said she didn't want anything fancy, she just wanted to see the players. You know she said if you started being clever and messing about with the lights, she'd have your guts for guitar strings.'

'She didn't mean it.'

'Yes, she did.' John leaned forward earnestly.

'What are you up to?'

'I just thought I'd add some atmosphere at the end. You know, the loud bit.'

John bit his lip. 'I don't think that's such a good idea.'

'Will you stop worrying.' Bright held up his hand to forestall John's protests as the music died away. 'Here we go.' He pressed the GO button on the lighting board.

The stage began to darken as the hushed

5

orchestra played a plaintive Russian folk melody. The clear white light was replaced by sombre blues and purples, giving the scene a mysterious and foreboding air. The players shifted nervously in their seats as their music grew dimmer before their eyes. Moving together as if hypnotized, they slowly leaned forward as the light faded until their noses were practically brushing the sheets on their music stands. The melody faltered. Ms Willis directed a fierce glare over her shoulder at the window of the lighting box.

John shook Bright's shoulder urgently. 'They can't see,' he hissed.

Bright smiled complacently as the unhappy musicians cast despairing glances at each other. 'Don't worry, it won't be for long. The loud bit's coming up. Then we'll see some fun.'

He reached over to the box with the Big Red Button, and turned the key. The LED display lit up. A word appeared on it in glowing red letters. It said, 'ARMED'. John crossed his fingers and shut his eyes.

'This is the bit where the bells and cannons come in, right?'

'Yes, the Russians are supposed to be

6

celebrating' said John. His eyes snapped open and his jaw dropped as a horrible suspicion dawned on him. 'Cannons,' he whispered. He grabbed Bright's shoulder. 'Bright ... you haven't ...?'

But the Russian winter was sweeping across the straggling remains of Napoleon's army. Bright pressed the GO button on the lighting board again, and the warm glow of dawn slowly flooded the stage. The players gave a sigh of relief as their scores became visible. The music became tense and urgent. Ms Willis beamed, willing the orchestra to a final all-out effort. Violin bows flying, trombone slides pumping, the musicians gathered themselves for the grand climax of the piece. With the orchestra in full cry, the joyous Russians swept to victory.

Bright's finger jabbed down on the Big Red Button ...

'It was only a small fire, sir.'

Bright's gaze was defiant as he stood facing the Head, who was flanked by two school governors. The governors had had the misfortune to be seated in the front row of the audience. Their ties were askew, their shirt fronts and faces blackened. Their eyebrows were singed and their hair was standing on end. They looked as if they had been caught in an explosion.

They had.

The Head breathed heavily through clenched teeth. 'Well, that's fine,' he said caustically. 'I'm sure that will be a great comfort to the survivors; to the cellists, for example, whose instruments you managed to burn to the ground.'

John glanced around nervously. Two of the cello players had joined the group surrounding Bright, still clutching the blackened remains of their instruments. They were giving Bright some very unfriendly looks.

'Or the brass player whose trombone caught the full force of the blast,' the Head went on. The trombonist glared at Bright. His trombone looked as if it had partially melted. He was clearly debating with himself how he could use the mangled instrument to do Bright the maximum amount of harm.

'A pretty comprehensive night's work, even for you.' The Head's fingers were twitching. He glanced over at the soot-blackened stage, where

several firemen were trying to extricate a flute player who had been blown into the bell of a tuba and whose head was now hopelessly stuck, and where paramedics were surrounding a woodwind player who had swallowed part of his oboe. 'The Mayor and Mayoress are being treated for shock, Ms Willis is under sedation and a dozen parents are threatening the school with legal action over damage to their eardrums.'

'I just wanted to put a few real explosions in for the cannons,' said Bright unrepentantly. 'I just didn't think they'd be that powerful,' he went on as the Head fought for self-control. John said nothing. He now knew what was in the box that Bright had brought from Dodgy Dave's Military Surplus Stores and had been trying to hide from him.

'They're just practice explosives,' said Bright. 'The army use them in exercises to give the men experience of being under fire. They're supposed to be safe,' he complained.

'*Safe!*' The Head choked with fury. 'They may be *safe* in the middle of Salisbury Plain, they're not designed to be *safe* in a school hall, for pity's sake.'

Bright regarded him sorrowfully. 'You're angry

with me, aren't you, sir?' he sighed. 'I can understand that.'

The Head fought for breath. 'You ...' With a visible effort, he controlled himself. He leaned forward and stared fixedly into Bright's eyes.

'I want to make something very clear to you,' he hissed through gritted teeth. 'You will never be allowed anywhere near the lighting or sound equipment ever again. I mean *ever*. You are barred from using that equipment until the heat death of the universe. Stars will burn themselves into cinders and Hell will freeze over before you lay a finger on so much as a pair of headphones.' He straightened his tie and went on in a more normal voice, 'I shall see you in my office at nine o'clock tomorrow, at which time I shall be very happy to make clear any part of this that you don't understand.'

Bright's eyes had grown wide with dismay. 'But, sir,' he protested, 'I can still do the school play, can't I? I'm supposed to be doing the lighting for ...'

The Head let out a strangled shriek. His face turned a strange colour. The governors standing

11

on either side stepped hurriedly in, seized him by the shoulders, and hustled him away.

Bright stared at the retreating figure and shook his head sadly.

'I'll take that as a "no" then,' he said.

CHAPTER TWO

Crisis Out of a **Drama**

'Enter Bright, stage left.'

The drama class turned as Bright stepped into the damp mobile hut that was ambitiously called the drama studio. It was painted black: black walls, black ceiling, black floor, black curtains. It looked like a crypt that had somehow ended up in a school, rather than in a graveyard.

Bright squinted into the darkness. Two dim spotlights lit up the circle of students who were gathered round Mr Henslowe, the drama teacher.

'Why are you so late, Vernon, dear boy? The lesson is nearly ended,' continued Mr Henslowe.

'I had to see the Head, sir,' explained Bright,

with a pained expression. True to his word, the Head had given Bright another roasting (though admittedly, this hadn't been as bad as the roasting Bright had given the orchestra).

As Bright took his place in the circle next to John, Mr Henslowe peered over his half-rimmed specs and chuckled. 'Ah yes, m'dear, I heard all about your exploits. That's what I call bringing the house down! You certainly made sure the concert went with a bang!' Mr Henslowe grinned toothily – the rivalry between the music and drama departments was well known.

'In fact, the evening will probably go down in history as the Last Night of the Bombs!' Mr Henslowe burst into a guffaw. There was a stony silence as the class shrugged their shoulders and shook their heads at the teacher's 'joke'.

Mr Henslowe's barking laughter came to an abrupt and embarrassed halt. 'Bombs – Proms, you see. It is a play on words,' he explained. The class remained blank-faced. Mr Henslowe tried once more. 'It's a pun.'

'Yeah, sir, but it's not punny!' piped up a voice.

The class burst into raucous laughter.

'All right, pipe down,' snapped Mr Henslowe.

After several more seconds of sniggers, the class obeyed. Mr Henslowe coughed. 'Now, Vernon, I was just reminding people about the rehearsal schedule for *Julius Caesar*. And I hope you've all learnt your lines!' Mr Henslowe glared pointedly at John, who began to go red.

Some members of the class were playing Plebeians, and their lines largely consisted of going 'rhubarb, rhubarb' during the crowd scenes, but John was playing the part of Lucius, the servant of Brutus. He'd decided to take part in the school production, or rather his mother had decided it for him. She thought it would 'be good' for him as it would 'help you to get to know more people'.

John had been at Elmley School for nearly a year. He'd moved when his mum and dad had split up. Although he'd settled down pretty well, he hadn't really made many friends, except for Bright. In fact, he probably hadn't made many new friends *because* of Bright.

Bright was brilliant at science. He was also good at football and cricket. He could get cricket balls to spin at incredible angles and could score goals at will. However, despite all his talents, Bright couldn't see (or perhaps didn't care) that

the self-satisfied way he displayed his own genius made most people want to strangle him on sight.

So, in order to keep the peace and his mum happy, John had presented himself at the auditions for the school production. Much to his surprise, he'd been given a named part. His little glow of self-congratulation hadn't lasted for long.

'You see,' Mr Henslowe had said, 'I need someone for this part who always looks slightly

bewildered – young, innocent, naïve, no mind of his own, easily led – in short, a bit dopey. You're absolutely perfect, dear boy!'

But the rehearsals had proved to be a struggle. Although Lucius wasn't a big part (Bright was constantly sneering at how few speeches John had), John found it difficult to learn the lines. What's more, he hadn't really met anyone through the production as his mum had hoped. Most of the other actors were from the upper school, and when they did speak to him, it was usually to complain about his giving them the wrong cues. The only person he regularly spoke to during rehearsals was Bright, who had volunteered to do the lighting.

As Mr Henslowe was still staring at him, John thought he'd better give the teacher the answer he wanted, even though it wasn't strictly true.

'Er, yes, I, er, I have,' he stammered. 'I'm, er, I'm, erm, word, er, perfect.'

The class burst out laughing and Mr Henslowe rolled his eyes heavenward. 'Of, er, course, er, you, er, are,' he said sarcastically before turning to Bright. 'I need a word with you. The rest of you get into groups of four. Prepare an improvisation involving conflict. Conflict of thought, person or place. Conflict is at the heart of great drama. The Bard's work is full of conflict. The Swan of Avon knew about conflict.'

'Isn't that the name of that pub in town that has a lot of punch-ups, sir?'

Mr Henslowe sadly shook his head. 'No, Terry, dear heart. I'm talking about Shakespeare.' He clapped his hands together. 'Let us get busy, busy, busy, m'dears. Time is money.'

As the class argued, bickered and organized themselves into working groups, Mr Henslowe turned to Bright. 'Now then, the Head has had a word with me about you. And I'm afraid it is not good news. For you, anyway,' he added. 'He has informed me that you are banned from lighting any more shows.'

'Yes, he sort of mentioned that to me,' said Bright, remembering the Head's bloodshot, staring eyes and foam-flecked lips as he had emphasized this point.

'So, I'm afraid you can't do the lighting for *Julius Caesar*. I'm going to ask Scholes in the sixth form to do it.'

Bright screwed his face up in protest. 'But he's useless, and I had some great ideas for it ...'

Mr Henslowe shook his head. 'I'm sorry, Bright. It's impossible. I can't defy the Head, dear boy, he'd blow a fuse – which coincidentally is exactly what you did the last time you lit a school production. In fact, you fused the whole school and half the town.'

'But I was only using the idea from the book on theatre history you lent me,' protested Bright. 'You know, wiring up the rapiers to the mains so that there'd be some realistic-looking sparks during the sword fight. And I got the wiring right, I'm almost positive ...'

'So were the poor actors who had to hold the swords,' Mr Henslowe pointed out. 'Almost positive, almost negative and almost electrocuted. I'm sorry, Bright, it's out of my hands.'

Mr Henslowe saw the look of disappointment on Bright's face and began to relent a little. After all, the sight of Ms Willis in the staff room that morning! Her perm would never be the same again. That would teach her to demand the hall for her music rehearsals when it was needed for drama rehearsals.

'I tell you what, dear boy, the ban only applies to lighting. Perhaps you could take charge of video recording the production? I'm sure even you can't cause any harm just pointing a video camera and pressing *record*,' said Mr Henslowe, showing a complete failure to understand that Bright was capable of causing unmitigated disaster with any piece of equipment more complicated than a spoon.

Bright sighed. Even he knew that the latest incident had pushed his credibility over the cliff.

'All right. I suppose I could …'

The conversation was brought to an abrupt end when a clattering of chairs and several loud yelps caused Mr Henslowe to spin round. Paul Adams and Terry McBride were in the process of trying to decapitate each other.

'What ho, you men, you beasts!' cried Mr Henslowe as he separated the two fighting bodies. 'What in blue blazes do you think you are doing!'

'It's conflict!' explained Terry, 'I was hitting him in role!'

Mr Henslowe shook his head. 'You blocks, you stones, you worse than senseless things!'

Before he could deliver further admonishment, the bell rang. There was a mad rush for the door. Mr Henslowe unsuccessfully tried to stem the flow, and settled for bellowing out instructions in the few seconds he had available.

'We'llseeyourworknextlesson.Caesarrehearsalt omorrowafterschooland … LEARN YOUR LINES!'

'My intelligence sources tell me there was a kinda big bang at your school yesterday p.m.,' drawled the man dressed in camouflaged combat gear.

'Nothin' to do with you, I suppose, Vernie?'

School had finished, and Bright and John now stood before David Thomas Vickers, who was better known as Dodgy Dave. Dave owned a military surplus store and supplied Bright with the various bits of gadgetry that he needed for his experiments. Some of these ex-military items were not strictly legal, nor were they strictly 'ex'. But Dave wasn't the type of person to let a couple of letters come between him and a customer.

Bright raised an eyebrow. 'Best not to suppose,' he replied firmly.

Dave nodded his head and tapped his nose. 'Like it, pardner. Information on a need-to-know basis – good thinkin'. If I don't know, I can't say. N to K – need to know. If the enemy capture me, I can't give nothin' away, cos I don't know nothin'. N to K!'

John wondered who on earth Dave thought the enemy was. Dodgy Dave lived in a world of his own most of the time. He was surrounded by military hardware, he dressed in combat gear, and he pretended that he'd fought in wars that had ended years before he'd been born.

Dave leaned conspiratorially towards Bright.

The overhead shop lights sparkled on his mirror sunglasses. 'But if, on the off chance, it might have been something to do with you, I hope you didn't reveal where you got the bang, bang material. I wouldn't want the enemy to get hold of that sort of information.'

'Don't worry, I didn't.' Bright nodded towards John, 'And neither did he.'

Dave straightened up. 'Sweet apple pie, boy, sweet apple pie!'

'Whatever,' replied Bright.

'So what can we load you up with? More big bang equipment? Finish the school off properly?!'

Bright shot Dave a death look.

'OK, amigo, my joke. N to K! N to K! So what's cookin' on the Vernie shoppin' list?'

Bright took out a notebook. 'I need some special video equipment. I've got to record the school production. Low levels of lighting. Some blackouts. Have you got any low-light video surveillance cameras? I was thinking of the type that the American special forces have been developing.'

Dave let out a long whistle. 'And how in thunderin' tarnation do you think I could get

23

hold of that sort of classified, top secret, multi-million dollar, hi-tech equipment?'

'The usual way, I suppose. Have you got any?'

Dave winked. 'How many do you need?'

CHAPTER THREE

What's the Time, Mister Wells?

'Not more rubbish!' Bright sighed in exasperation. John pulled a video from his bag.

'It's not rubbish,' protested John. 'It's *The Time Machine* by H.G. Wells. It's a classic.'

'Classic rubbish,' muttered Bright sourly.

They were in Bright's sitting room the following evening. John had called round on his way home from the *Julius Caesar* rehearsal, during which he had forgotten even more lines than usual. Bright, in a fit of the sulks, had refused to attend, but he had demanded a blow-by-blow account from John. Now it was John's turn to choose a video, and he'd brought a science-fiction movie.

For all his interest in science, Bright couldn't stand science fiction. John had once gone to the cinema with Bright to see *Star Wars* and had vowed 'never again'.

Bright had insisted on laughing derisively and making disparaging comments all the way through the film. 'Listen to the noise those spaceships are making,' he had complained during a spectacular battle among the stars. 'That's not possible! Space is a vacuum! How are those ships supposed to make *verrrrooooouuunn* noises when there's no air to carry the sound waves?'

'Will you shut up?' a voice behind them had said for the umpteenth time.

'You can't have a battle with no noises,' John had hissed, 'it wouldn't be exciting.'

Bright had taken no notice and hooted at the screen. 'Unscientific nonsense! Rubbish! Tripe! Codswallop! Balderdash!' He'd only been silenced when the irritated punter sitting behind him had dumped a tub of popcorn over his head.

John loved science fiction. He loved the sense of adventure, the endless possibilities. The more gadgetry and explosions involved, the better. Who cared about scientific accuracy when there were new worlds to conquer?

Bright picked up the video case and stared scornfully at the picture of the time machine on the cover. 'What's that supposed to be? Look at it! It looks like a bathtub with a golfing umbrella stuck to the back. How's that supposed to work?' He handed it back to John with contempt. 'You couldn't travel in time in a thing like that. It's ridiculous.'

John sighed. He'd known perfectly well how Bright would react to the film. Why did he keep trying?

'I wouldn't mind going back in time a couple of weeks,' he said placatingly. 'That way I'd stand a chance of learning my lines for the play – I always say them in the wrong place.'

Bright was in a bad mood. 'You've hardly got any lines,' he sneered. 'Anyway, the universe doesn't work like that. Time travel is impossible. The only way you could even *look* into the past would be to travel faster than the speed of light.'

John's forehead creased with the effort of thought. 'What's light got to do with it?'

'The speed of light is fixed,' Bright explained with weary patience. 'Everything else is relative.' John looked blank. Bright sighed heavily. 'Look, have you ever looked out of the window of a train and thought, "Hey, the station platform is moving!"?'

John nodded slowly.

'That's because you didn't feel the train start to move, and you know you're not moving inside the train, so just for a second your brain says, "It must be the platform that's moving," before common sense cuts in and reminds you that stations don't move.'

John nodded again.

'That's what Einstein's Theory of Relativity is all about. Everything is relative – mass, size, speed – it all depends on where you are and how fast you're going in relation to everything else.'

'All rrriiight …' said John cautiously.

'But light always moves at three-hundred-thousand kilometres per second, if we ignore the effect of gravity. I think we can ignore gravity for now, don't you?'

'Yes please,' said John fervently.

'It doesn't matter where you are in the universe or what direction you're moving in. Got that?'

'Yeeessss …'

'Good. Now, the further away from us a star is, the longer its light takes to reach us here on Earth. Even the light from the sun takes eight minutes. If the sun blew up right now, we'd have plenty of time to make a nice cup of tea – not knowing we'd be vaporized before we could drink it.'

John surreptitiously twitched the curtain aside and glanced out at the setting sun. It looked all right. But then it would, wouldn't it? Supposing it had blown up? What could he do with his last eight minutes of life? He didn't even like tea! John realized that Bright was watching him with a knowing smile. He let the curtain go and made an effort to look unconcerned.

'The distance between stars is huge,' Bright went on. 'If you try to work it out in miles or kilometres, you just end up with rows of noughts. So we measure the distance from Earth to the stars in light years, which is the distance a beam of light travels in one whole year.'

John screwed up his eyes as he tried to work

out how far a light year was in his head. Three-hundred-thousand kilometres per second, times sixty seconds per minute, times sixty minutes per hour, times twenty-four hours per day, times three-hundred-and-sixty-five-and-a-quarter days per year ... his head began to ache.

'So,' Bright continued, 'when we look at a star five hundred light years away from us, we're not seeing it as it is now. We're seeing it as it was five hundred years ago, because the light from it has taken five hundred years to get here. It might have blown up in the meantime – what we're looking at may no longer exist.'

So that's a bit more than a billion kilometres an hour, thought John, provided I've got the decimal point in the right place, and nearly twenty-six billion kilometres a day ...

'On the other hand,' Bright rattled on, 'suppose the star hasn't blown up, and suppose you could travel to it instantly. In that case, the light from Earth that was just reaching that star would have left here five hundred years ago. So if you had a big enough telescope, you would be able to see what was happening on Earth in Tudor times.'

'Aha!' John gave up trying to multiply twenty-six billion by three hundred and sixty-five and a quarter, and pointed a triumphant finger at Bright. 'So time travel *is* possible ...'

'I said you could *see* what was happening five hundred years ago,' Bright pointed out. 'I never said you could *go* there. In any case, even seeing into the Earth's past is impossible. Remember, I said you'd have to get to the star instantly. You'd have to travel there five hundred times faster than the speed of light, and that can't be done.'

'Why not?' objected John. For the space travellers in his favourite films and TV shows, travelling faster than light was as easy as hopping on a bus. 'What about hyperdrives?'

Bright shook his head in exasperation. 'They're always going on in films about hyperdrives and warp drives and things. It's all a load of rubbish. Light is the fastest thing in the universe. Nothing can travel faster than light.'

'Why not?' John demanded again.

'It's very complicated,' drawled Bright, with a maddening air of superiority. 'I don't know whether you'd understand.'

John gritted his teeth. 'Let's find out, shall we?'

'All right.' Bright leaned across to the fruit

bowl on the sideboard and picked up an apple. 'This apple has mass. That's to say, it's a solid object. You could put it in a set of scales and weigh it. Now, suppose you could make this apple move faster and faster until it was moving at the speed of light. What would happen?'

'You'd have the world's first intergalactic Golden Delicious?'

Bright clicked his tongue in annoyance. 'No. What would happen is that its mass would increase until this apple had more mass than the entire universe.'

John stared at the apple. It was a bit wrinkled and didn't look very nice. 'You're having me on.'

'It's true. If you put this apple into one side of a set of scales, and all the stars and planets in the universe in the other, the apple would weigh more.'

John whistled. 'You'd need a very big set of scales.'

'I was speaking metaphorically!' snapped Bright.

'I was joking,' said John wearily.

'Oh, right. Anyway, the important thing,' Bright went on, 'is that you couldn't get the apple to travel at the speed of light anyway.'

'Why not?'

'Because you'd need an infinite force to do it.'

'So?' John crouched down to put the video into the player.

'So there's no such thing as an infinite force. Look, if I kick your backside …'

'Ow!'

'That's a force. I use energy to make the kick and the force of the kick sends you forwards.'

'That hurt!' John rubbed his nose where he'd banged it nosediving into the carpet.

'But that's just a tiny force.'

John flexed his foot experimentally. 'Let's see if I can show you a bigger one.'

'The point is, an infinite force would be bigger than any force that has ever existed. Bigger than the Big Bang that started the universe. It's an impossibility.'

'But just a minute,' John objected. He grimaced as he tried to get his thoughts in order. 'If anything that travels at the speed of light has infinite mass, and needs an infinite force to get it up to the speed of light, how can *light* travel at the speed of light?' He grinned and sat back to enjoy watching Bright try to get out of that one.

Bright clicked his tongue in exasperation. 'I knew you weren't paying attention. I said anything that has *mass* becomes infinitely massive at the speed of light. But light is made up of photons, and photons have no mass.' He took a bite out of the apple and chewed it thoughtfully. 'There are lots of other effects that make time travel impractical, things like time-dilation, dimensional fluctuations ...'

'Stop! My brain's going to explode!' John shook his head in confusion.

Bright gave him a patronizing smile and patted him on the shoulder. 'Just take my word for it. Forget about time travel. There's no such thing.' Bright sat back on the sofa. 'Well, go on then. Are we going to watch this *Time Machine* video of yours?'

'I don't think so.' John sighed and put the video back in his bag. 'Do you know, for some reason I've completely gone off the whole idea.' He dragged a dog-eared copy of *Julius Caesar* out of the bag. 'Come on, you can help me learn my lines instead. I've been trying to avoid doing this for ages.'

Bright stretched. 'All right,' he said.

John threw the book to Bright, who nonchalantly plucked it out of the air, one-handed.

'If I haven't got them learned for next week, Mr Henslowe has promised to do to me what Brutus did to Caesar.'

'What did he do?'

'He stabbed him in the forum.' John thought for a moment. 'And the behind'em. And all over'em, come to that.'

'Sounds painful,' said Bright. 'All right, I'll help – but only if you agree to help me out with setting up the video equipment.'

'Deal,' John agreed casually, not having the slightest inkling what the future had in store for him.

Yet.

Which was just as well.

CHAPTER FOUR

Bright's Out-of-Sight Light

A few days later, John and Bright headed down a flight of stone steps to Bright's laboratory in the cellar. It was full of strange-looking electronic gizmos, glass jars, bits of wire and anything else you would associate with a mad scientist's playroom. The lab had been put together by Bright's father, but was mainly used by Bright.

John had never met Bright's father. As a top scientist he was always away on special missions for the Government, working on new ways to stop mad scientists from other countries blowing up the world. For some reason (according to Bright), this usually involved thinking of new ways of blowing up the world himself.

As he entered the lab John gave a cheery wave to Horace, Bright's laboratory guinea pig. Horace returned John's greeting with a look of panic. A small part of his guinea-pig brain reminded him that whenever Bright and John got together in the lab something bad usually happened.

Bright pointed to a pile of boxes. They were marked in bold black lettering, which said things like:

MOST TOP SECRET, PROPERTY OF THE STATE DEPT

and …

FOR THE ATTENTION OF MI6.

'Dave delivered these earlier,' breezed Bright as he began opening the cases. 'This is real sci-fi equipment,' he gloated. 'Not like the rubbish you see in your films that doesn't exist and never will.'

John stared at the gleaming cameras and computer boxes. 'These look brand new!' he exclaimed. 'How does Dave get hold of this stuff?'

Bright smiled. 'I don't ask, he doesn't answer.'

'N to K?' nodded John.

'Exactly,' agreed Bright.

A week went by. John spent most of the evenings when he wasn't rehearsing 'helping' Bright, though most of what Bright was doing was so complicated that John's contribution seemed to consist mostly of getting cans of cola from the fridge and holding things. Then he was called for several rehearsals in a row and lost track of what Bright was up to.

One day after school, Bright grabbed John's sleeve as they spilled out into the corridor.

'Can you come round tonight?' he asked.

John nodded. 'They're doing Act One tonight. I'm not in that.'

'Good. I've got something to show you.'

John eyed him warily. 'Oh? What?'

Bright winked mysteriously. 'Aha!'

John groaned inwardly. Where had he heard that before?

*

John stared at the apparatus in Bright's living room.

'All right,' he said after some time, 'what is it?'

Bright's grin was a fifty-fifty mixture of pride and conceit. 'Well,' he said, 'that's the camera …'

'I know that,' snapped John. 'Even I can recognize a camera when I see one. I meant, what's *this*?'

He pointed to a steel box with its cover off and

complicated bits hanging out. It was connected to the camera and had a satellite dish on top.

'That's the transmitter,' said Bright. 'Follow me.'

He led the way through the kitchen and down the steps to his laboratory.

'And *this* ...' he said, indicating another box, covered with a mind-boggling array of dials and switches, 'is the receiver.'

John stared at it. 'What does it receive?'

Bright put his head close to John's and said, very slowly and clearly, 'Whatever – we – send – from – the – transmitter.'

John still looked blank. Bright gave a theatrical sigh.

'Eventually, I'll have several cameras feeding into the transmitter,' he explained. 'The transmitter codes the pictures from the cameras into digital signals, and sends them up to a communications' satellite.'

'Communications' satellite,' repeated John dazedly.

Bright nodded. 'There are dozens of them up there, circling the globe. The satellite bounces the signal back down. It's picked up by the dish on the roof and fed down here to the receiver and then on to the DVD recorder just here. We can monitor it all on this VDU,' he concluded.

A familiar feeling began to enter John's head. A dull throbbing ache. It always happened when Bright was explaining something and John hadn't really got a clue what he was going on about.

'Are you allowed to use a communications' satellite just like that?' he objected.

Bright waved this aside. 'It belongs to my dad's people,' he said airily. 'I have the codes.'

John noted that Bright hadn't actually answered his question.

'But isn't this all a bit over the top?' he asked. 'Why don't you just use a couple of normal cameras and cables? Why make it so complicated?'

'To push back the boundaries of human capability.' Bright looked astonished that even John could ask something to which the answer was so blindingly obvious. 'I thought you liked sci-fi,' he went on accusingly. 'You know, "to go boldly where no one has ever boldly gone ever before … er … boldly." That's what I'm doing.'

'That's not quite right. It's actually, "to boldly …"'

'It doesn't matter what it is. The point is that we have to try to advance science and technology. I mean, where would we be if Einstein hadn't thought about relativity?' said Bright, tutting.

43

'We wouldn't have atomic bombs and the power to blow up the world!' John snapped back.

Bright gave John a pitying stare. 'Why do you have to be so negative and see the worst in everything?'

'Because it needs people like me to tell people like you that just because you can do something, it doesn't mean you *should* do it if doing it means ... er ... I mean, if it would cause ... that is ...' John faltered to a stop. 'Well, you know what I mean,' he said lamely.

From the look that he gave John, Bright clearly didn't.

'Well, for instance, what about some of your experiments?'

Bright winced. John had hit a sore point. It was true – some of Bright's experiments hadn't gone according to plan.

'There are always going to be some initial teething problems when pushing back the boundaries,' he said haughtily.

John felt a great weariness wash over him. Arguing with Bright always seemed to have that effect. 'All right. How does it work?'

Bright reached into a box and carefully pulled out a camera. 'It's all to do with light. Right?'

'Yes, Bright.'

Bright gave John a sour look. 'Light,' he said, 'is made up of particles of energy called photons. Photons travel in waves.'

'You mean, like waves on the sea?'

'More or less. But there are lots of different types of waves. Short, choppy ones; long rolling ones. Some colours of light have long wavelengths, some have short ...' Bright paused as he realized that John was standing stock still with a trance-like expression on his face. He snapped his fingers. John jumped.

'Did you follow that?'

'Of course not,' admitted John. 'I lost you at the seaside. I was thinking about sandcastles and ice creams.'

'Within visible light,' Bright went on with studied patience, 'all the different colours have their own wavelengths ...'

'Like the colours you get from a prism?' said John eagerly, remembering half-digested science lessons, 'or a rainbow?'

'Exactly. A prism splits visible light into its

different wavelengths. That means we can see the different colours. For example, red has a longer wavelength than blue. So there you are. Richard Of York Gave Battle In Vain.'

John stared at Bright. 'Did he?'

Bright clicked his tongue. 'That's how you remember the colours. Red – Orange – Yellow – Green – Blue – Indigo – Violet. R – O – Y – G – B – I – V. Richard Of York Gave Battle In Vain.'

'So you keep saying.'

'The point *is*,' said Bright loudly, 'that this camera sends the picture to the transmitter. The transmitter converts the picture into a digital signal – or rather, three signals: one for red, one for green and one for blue, the three primary colours of the spectrum. The signals are then transformed to a much higher wavelength. Then they're sent, via the satellite, back down here to the receiver and on to the VDU! Simple.'

'Only for someone with a brain the size of China,' said John.

'That'll be me!' replied Bright matter-of-factly. Then his face fell. 'The trouble is, I'm running out of time,' he admitted. 'The dress rehearsal is only a couple of weeks away, and I have to have everything installed by then, so I want to get this test-rig working tonight. But I haven't finished putting together the transmitter yet.'

John shrugged. 'I'll do some soldering for you, if you like.'

Bright gave him the sort of look most other people reserved for something nasty they'd found on the sole of their shoe. 'You?' he said with undisguised contempt.

John flushed angrily. 'Yes, me! I'm not *totally* useless, you know.'

'Of course not,' said Bright hurriedly. 'Not *totally* ...'

John reached across the bench and grabbed the soldering iron. 'Go on, then – try me.'

Bright gave him a worried look. 'Well, if you follow the diagram, I suppose even you can't go too far wrong ...' He hesitated a moment longer. 'Oh, all right.' He led John up the stairs and back to the living room. John plugged the soldering iron into a wall socket while Bright took several bits out of a box marked TOP SECRET.

'You need to solder that bit to that,' said Bright, pointing to a space on a circuit board inside the machine. He handed John a piece of paper covered with indecipherable squiggles. 'There's a diagram.'

'Right,' said John grimly, 'leave it to me.'

'OK – er – I've got to make some adjustments to the receiver.' Bright shifted his weight nervously from foot to foot. 'Just call me if you need anything, OK?'

John, studying the diagram, grunted.

With many worried backward glances, Bright crossed the room. As he reached the door he turned and said, 'Are you sure …?'

'I said, leave it to me!'

'Right, right.' Looking far from happy, Bright wandered out.

Left alone, John's bravado evaporated. He knew nothing about electronics, and very little more about soldering. Then he squared his shoulders. He was fed up with being pushed around. Who did Bright think he was? 'I'll show him,' he muttered. 'How hard can it be?'

Fifteen minutes later, John had sunk to the depths of despair. What was supposed to go in now? Was it this bit or that bit? And did it go in here or there? John stared helplessly at the diagram. Oh no! He'd been looking at it upside down! Frantically he began to pull wires off circuit boards and fix them back in the right place. Or at least he hoped they were back in the right place ...

John pushed the last circuit board into its slot. He put the top back on the box. He prayed a little prayer.

Bright came in. 'All done? Good.' He crossed to the camera and began to adjust it. 'Switch it on, then nip down to the lab and turn on the receiver and recorder, would you?'

John pressed the power switch on the transmitter. A green light came on. At least it hadn't exploded. With fingers crossed, John went down to the cellar, switched on the receiver and set the DVD to record. He turned to look at the VDU. Lines of static flashed across the monitor screen. I knew it, John told himself. I knew I'd mess something up. Look at it! Hopeless! He was just about to turn the machine off when, to his amazement, an image began to form. There, on the monitor, was Bright.

'It works! Yehaaah!' John punched the air in triumph ... and suddenly stopped and gazed at the monitor in disbelief. His jaw dropped. He leaned closer and stared blankly at the screen …

… as the figure of John Watt appeared in the picture and grabbed Bright by the arm.

On the screen, Bright spun round and stared at the John in the picture. 'What on earth are you doing here? You're supposed to be by the receiver.'

The John in the picture stopped dead. 'That's what you said just now!'

'What?' Bright was clearly nonplussed. John's head was spinning. Not only was he in two places at once, he was talking gibberish.

'Calm down,' Bright soothed, 'and tell me what you're talking about.'

'You said that too!' The John in the picture suddenly clapped a hand to his mouth and giggled. 'And now I'm saying what I said!' He pointed a triumphant finger at Bright. 'I even know what you're going to say next!'

'Have you gone stark, staring, raving mad?' Bright and the John in the picture said together.

The John in the picture did a little dance of glee. 'This is weird. This is weirder than a weird afternoon in Weirdsville.' He laughed at the expression of disbelieving horror on Bright's face. 'Come on, I'll show you.'

Bright and the other John disappeared from the picture.

With a gasp of disbelief, John tore himself away from the monitor and raced up the cellar steps.

CHAPTER FIVE

A Can of Wormholes

John dashed into the living room and grabbed Bright by the arm. Bright spun round and stared at him. 'What on earth are you doing here? You're supposed to be by the receiver.'

John stared at him in disbelief. 'That's what you said just now!'

'What?' Bright stared at him in confusion. 'Calm down and tell me what you're talking about.'

'You said that too!' John clapped a hand to his mouth. He and Bright were replaying the conversation he had just seen on the VDU screen, word for word. He giggled. 'And now I'm saying what I said!' A thought struck him. For once he knew something that Bright didn't know. 'I even know what you're going to say next!' he told Bright. As Bright opened his mouth, John spoke simultaneously …

'Have you gone stark, staring, raving mad?' they both said together.

John could barely contain himself. He hopped around in excitement. 'This is weird. This is weirder than a weird afternoon in Weirdsville.' He looked at Bright's face and burst out laughing. 'Come on, I'll show you.'

Back in the cellar, John checked the recorder. It was still recording, but now the VDU screen was blank. Bright stared at it. 'So?'

John held up a finger to silence Bright. Then he reset the DVD to the start of the recording.

A picture appeared. On the screen, John dashed into the living room and grabbed Bright by the arm. Bright spun round and stared at him. 'What on earth are you doing here? You're supposed to be by the receiver …'

The recording played itself out. Bright stared at it.

'OK, so you recorded yourself being strange,' he said cuttingly. 'I still don't see what …'

'The point is,' John said very loudly and very slowly, 'I saw all that happen and recorded it before it happened.'

Bright stared at him. To John's secret delight, a look of complete bafflement spread across Bright's face. He licked his lips.

'Just run that by me again,' he said.

John did.

Bright groaned. Then he turned on his heel and rushed upstairs.

Back in the living room, Bright tore the cover off the transmitter and stared at the bird's nest of wiring John had made inside. He gave a scream of rage.

'Look at it!' he yelled. 'I knew I shouldn't have left you to do it. I knew you'd make a mess of it, you clumsy, half-witted apology for a short-sighted baboon with two left hands! What have you done?'

'I don't know!' John was thoroughly enjoying Bright's confusion.

Bright buried his head in his hands. 'Use logic,' he muttered to himself. 'How can you record something that's happened – will happen – will have happened – in the future? ... Particles ... faster than light ... impossible ... speed ...'

Suddenly Bright looked up. His eyes widened. 'If what you say is true …' He began to quiver with excitement. 'Somehow, we've looked into the future and recorded it!'

'Wait a minute,' said John as he followed Bright down the stairs into the cellar. 'You're saying that the recorder is receiving pictures from the camera before the transmitter actually sends them because the pictures are travelling faster than the speed of light?'

Eyes gleaming with excitement, Bright nodded.

'But you said that was impossible!'

Bright shrugged dismissively. 'I've been wrong before.' He thought for a moment. 'Three years ago, a Tuesday afternoon in February …'

'So why is it happening?' John interrupted.

'I don't know.' Bright shook his head in frustration. 'I know what it's doing, I just don't know how it's doing it.' He thought for a moment, then snapped his fingers decisively. 'Wormholes!'

'Same to you.'

'No, no, no!' Bright waved his arms about

excitedly. 'That could be what's happening. Whatever particles the transmitter is sending out may be creating their own wormholes.'

John gave a moan. 'You're about to explain something that's going to turn my brain into jelly again, aren't you?'

'Oh, wormholes are perfectly simple.'

It was John's turn to bury his face in his hands.

'A wormhole,' said Bright, 'is a short cut across the space–time continuum.'

John's voice was muffled. 'Yes,' he said, 'I can definitely feel my brain wobbling. Wobble, wobble, wobble ...'

'Scientists believe that tiny wormholes can occur naturally in space time, but they don't know much about them yet.' Bright reached for an apple that he had set aside for Horace. The guinea pig squeaked indignantly. 'Look, take this apple ...'

John gave Bright a hunted look. 'Not more apples!' he implored.

'If an apple was good enough for Isaac Newton, it's good enough for you.' Bright took out a ballpoint pen and made two marks on opposite sides of the apple, which he then labelled A and B. 'Now, suppose you had to travel from point A to point B. What would be the quickest way? Round the outside of the apple, or straight through the middle of it?'

'Well, through the middle of course, but ...'

'So, if an ant and a worm set off together from point A to point B, and the ant went round the outside of the apple and the worm tunnelled straight through it, and they were travelling at the same speed, which would get there first?'

'Well, the worm would because ... ah. I see.'

'Exactly. If the outside of the apple is normal space, then the wormhole goes through somewhere else. You could call it sub-space ...'

'Or hyper-space?' suggested John.

'It doesn't matter,' Bright snapped back. 'The point is that the particles produced by my machine may not be travelling faster than light at all. They may be creating their own wormholes and bypassing the laws of the physical universe. They could be shooting off on an unimaginable journey through space–time and arriving back on Earth before they have actually been sent. In other words, the transmitter is sending pictures from the camera back into the past. I must find out how!' Bright concluded, his eyes shining with the light of scientific inquiry.

'Oh yes?' said John warily. 'And how are you going to do that?'

Bright was already reaching for the soldering iron. 'I'll have to take the transmitter apart and then ...'

John placed a restraining hand on Bright's sleeve. Speaking very slowly and clearly, he said, 'Before you do that, I think you'd better make very sure that you can put it back together again, don't you?'

Bright dropped the soldering iron with a clatter.

'Exactly,' John went on. 'I don't know why this thing is doing what it's doing, and neither do you. If you take it apart, you might find out. But you might not, and then where would you be? I can't remember which bits I stuck to what, or what order I stuck them in. We could spend for ever trying to duplicate what I did.'

'But in order to find out what happened, I have to take the machine apart. But taking it apart will probably destroy whatever is causing the faster-than-light effect, and that could be anything!'

Bright's face was white. 'But I must know what happened. My machine has the power to change the world!'

John glared at him. 'What do you mean, *your* machine?'

'What do you mean, what do I mean?'

'It's my machine as much as yours,' John pointed out hotly. 'I put the final pieces in place, didn't I? I did the soldering. Whatever this machine is doing that it shouldn't be doing, is because of something I did.'

Bright's voice became oily. 'And don't think I don't recognize and appreciate your efforts ...'

'You said I was a clumsy, half-witted apology for a short-sighted baboon with two left hands.'

'Well, yes, but I was speaking figuratively.'

John didn't want Bright to know that he didn't know what figuratively meant. 'Oh, well, that's all right then.'

Bright rubbed his hands together and chuckled gleefully. 'It's amazing how many great scientific discoveries have happened purely by chance,' he enthused. 'Take James Watt for instance.'

John gave him a puzzled look. 'My grandad?'

Bright tutted. 'No, no, no – another James Watt,

a Scottish engineer. He watched a kettle boiling and came up with the idea of ...'

'... a cup of tea?' suggested John helpfully.

'The steam engine,' snapped Bright. 'Then there was Alexander Fleming who accidentally let mould grow on a culture dish and discovered penicillin ...'

'... and Herr E. Sausage, who left a plate of rabbit droppings, rotten cabbage and sheeps' brains out in the rain overnight, and in the morning realized that he had invented school dinners.'

Bright regarded John sorrowfully. 'You're not taking this seriously, are you?'

Frustrated in his wish to take the transmitter apart, Bright insisted on doing some experiments immediately to find out just how far into the future they could see.

Bright switched on the receiver again. Immediately, the picture showed a clock. It was a rather fancy digital clock with big white numbers.

'That's my alarm clock,' said Bright, staring at it.

John checked the time on his watch. 7.20 p.m. The clock said it was 7.25.

Bright stampeded upstairs and fetched the clock from his bedroom. He and John set it up in front of the camera in the living room and, with the time on the clock showing 7.25 p.m., switched the transmitter on.

'So we're looking five minutes into the future.' Bright pursed his lips. 'Not very far … I wonder …'

He switched the transmitter off and unplugged it. Then he took the cover off and started fiddling around inside.

'Watch out!' said John. 'You'll ruin it.'

'I don't think so.' Bright looked up briefly. 'I'm not taking anything apart, just changing the power settings.'

Bright spent some time making further adjustments before he grunted with satisfaction and replaced the cover.

'Let's see what that does,' he said, and switched the transmitter back on.

He and John pelted back down the cellar steps into the lab. Bright checked the clock on the TV screen. The time on it read 8.45. They raced back to the living room. John

checked his watch against the time on the clock. The time was 7.40.

'Just over an hour!' Bright was jubilant. 'I thought so! When I increase the power, the signal from the transmitter travels faster – or goes on a different journey. Either way, the result is the same.'

He opened a drawer and fished out a calculator. Tapping numbers into it, he kept up a broken commentary. 'Now, I boosted the power by ... and that gave me ... so if I rack the power output up to ... that should result in ...' He gave a triumphant chortle. 'I reckon that if I run this set-up on maximum power, we should be able to look about thirty-six hours into the future!'

'Oh.' John was disappointed. 'That doesn't sound like much.'

'But this is only the start!' Bright was practically dancing with glee. 'Once we've found out how the machine works, we can make it more powerful and more efficient. Who knows? We might be able to look years into the future! Hundreds of years! Maybe thousands!'

'Aren't you getting a bit carried away?' John shook his head doubtfully. 'That far in the future, we won't even be alive any more. Who's going to operate the camera and send pictures back into the past then?'

'Details!' snapped Bright. 'Mere details! We'll work something out. By that time, my position in the history of scientific development will be secure. My name will live for ever!'

'Oh, *your* name will live for ever, will it? That's nice,' said John sarcastically.

'Books will be written about me!'

'Lovely.'

Bright gave John a patronizing smile. 'I'll make sure you get mentioned in the footnotes, of course.'

'Oh, thanks ever so.'

'Of course, this new particle will be named after me,' said Bright with a smirk. 'Lots of people have their names remembered that way. Volts are named after Alessandro Volta, and amps after André Ampère ...'

'And kilos after Baron Ludwig von Kilogram, and tonnes after Enrico Tonne, the overweight opera singer,' said John cuttingly.

The joke was wasted on Bright. 'Exactly! So it's only fair that this discovery should be named after me. I shall call these new particles ...' he hesitated for dramatic effect, then struck a pose and cried in ringing tones, "Brightons!"'

John stared at him in disbelief. 'You're totally cracked, you know that, don't you?'

Bright was hurt. 'Why? What's wrong with that?'

'Well, for starters, Brighton isn't a sub-atomic particle, it's a place by the seaside.'

'But I've got to call them "something-on",' Bright said plaintively. 'All those sorts of particles end in -on. There's the proton, the neutron, the electron, the photon ...'

A wicked gleam crept into John's eyes. 'Of course, you have to call them something that ends with -on. I can see that. Why don't you call them *Vernons*?'

A spasm of pain passed across Bright's face. He hated his first name. He bit his lip, took the cover off the transmitter again, and delved deep into its electronic innards.

'Are you going to get it to produce more *Vernons* then?' asked John sweetly.

Bright raised his head just long enough to give John a quelling look. 'I've had second thoughts about the whole naming business.' He turned his attention back to the transmitter and his voice became muffled. 'Sometimes, the price of fame can be just too high ...'

A few minutes later, Bright slotted the cover back on the machine and switched it on. 'Right. I've boosted all the power links. The next time we transmit a picture from the camera, it should send it about twenty-four hours into the past. In other words, any picture that we receive now should come from about this time tomorrow.'

'O-Kaaaaay ...' said John uncertainly.

'Just take my word for it.'

They raced back to the cellar and switched the DVD recorder on. The TV screen cleared to show an image. Bright and John watched with bated breath as a hand came into shot, holding a newspaper with the date circled in biro.

'That's tomorrow's paper.' Bright rubbed his hands together. 'So far, so good ...'

The scene changed. The picture showed a scuffed, nondescript passageway with lockers along one side.

'That's at our school,' exclaimed John, recognizing some of the peeling artwork on the walls. 'It's the corridor outside the art rooms.'

The camera jolted. It inched left and right and came to rest on a bored-looking girl in the centre of the frame. She was leaning against a wall and twisting a loop of hair between her fingers.

'That's Vicky Savage,' said Bright. 'She's in Year Nine.'

As he spent most of his time in school with Bright, John didn't often get to hear school

gossip, but he was vaguely aware that Vicky Savage was known to go out only with boys in Year 11 or higher, and only then if they had a moped.

'And that,' said Bright as a nervous-looking boy moving with ill-feigned nonchalance wandered into the frame, 'is Mick Philips from our year.' He gave an unpleasant grin and leaned forward, narrowing his eyes. 'Now this *does* look interesting ...'

CHAPTER SIX

A Savage Encounter

'What do you mean, I shouldn't ask Vicky Savage out?' said Mick Philips.

'Because it will all go horribly wrong,' said Bright with a knowing smile. 'Trust me.'

Mick Philips had been puzzled when Bright had sidled over to him at morning registration and hissed, 'Mick, just a word in your ear.'

Mick was puzzled because Bright didn't often speak to him. In fact Mick could never remember an occasion when Bright *had* spoken to him. They were more different than chalk and cheese, which at least began with the same two letters. Bright and Mick weren't even in the same alphabet.

Bright could be pricklier than a hedgehog doing needlework, whereas Mick Philips was as smooth as a fishmonger's slab, and twice as cool. He dressed in all the best designer gear. He knew which labels were in, which ones were out, and what was taking off, going down or coming back. Bright, on the other hand, dressed like a dead sheep.

Bright's interest in girls went as far as understanding that they were biologically different from boys. In stark contrast, Mick Philips was God's gift to women. Or so Mick Philips thought. If girls fancied Mick as much as he fancied himself, they'd have to form a queue three times round the planet.

So it had come as a bit of a shock to Mick when Bright had whispered in his ear, 'Whatever you do, don't ask Vicky Savage to go out with you.'

Mick was annoyed because he had never given Vicky Savage a moment's thought. Mind you, if he had, there was no way that Vicky Savage would be able to resist his charms. Or so Mick believed.

'Trust me ...' repeated Bright.

Mick narrowed his eyes. 'Is this a wind-up?'

He glanced over Bright's shoulder and saw John grinning stupidly and signalling 'no' like a noddy-dog on a trampoline.

Terry McBride and a group of his associates began to gather round. 'What's up, Mick?' asked Terry.

'Bright Light here reckons I shouldn't ask Vicky Savage out,' replied Mick.

'Vicky Savage?' Terry whistled. 'She'd have you on toast.'

Mick drew himself up. 'Says who?' He turned to Bright. 'Is that what you're saying? I'm not good enough for her?'

'No,' said Bright, 'I'm merely saying that you shouldn't ask her out because something bad will happen to you.'

Mick glared hard at Bright. 'Fortune-teller, are you?'

A hint of a smile flickered across Bright's face. 'Sort of …'

John couldn't have explained exactly why he had a bad feeling about Bright's meddling, but he felt he ought to support Mick. 'Bright's only talking about what *would* happen if you asked Vicky out, Mick. Nobody's saying you have to ask her out …' He tailed off as he noticed the nasty grin on Terry's face, and Bright's dagger-stare. 'I mean … er … if you don't want to … er … I mean, it's your decision …' he mumbled.

'Yeah, you *don't* have to, Mick,' said Terry, laughing, as he began to flap his arms up and down. 'It's *your* decision …' The group of lads began to join in with the arm flapping. 'Squawk, squawk, cluck cluck!'

Mick clenched his fists in defiance. 'All right, I'll do it!'

Bright was still smiling the smile of a wide-mouthed frog as he and John headed towards first lesson.

'Thanks for your help there, that tipped the scales,' breezed Bright.

'I wasn't trying to,' moaned John.

'Now, all you've got to do is film the moment when he asks her out.'

'Why me?' John protested.

Bright raised an eyebrow. 'I thought you wanted recognition for this invention,' he said pointedly. 'You are going to be the first person to record the future. You'll be famous!'

John gave him a sideways glance. 'Oh yes?'

'Yes,' repeated Bright. 'You'll go down in history. Just like the man who helped Alexander Graham Bell when he invented the telephone.'

'What did he do?'

'He sat in a room and he heard Bell's voice on the telephone, telling him to come next door, and he went. That's why he's famous.'

'What did Bell want him for?'

Bright gave John an exasperated look. 'I don't know! It doesn't matter. I don't suppose he wanted him for anything at all, really …'

'So why did he call him then?'

'The point is,' said Bright, breathing deeply, 'Bell called him on the telephone. He was the first person in history to get a telephone call!'

'And what was this bloke's name?' asked John deliberately.

'I can't remember.'

'Exactly!'

'Stop being picky!' ordered Bright. 'Anyway, I've got to make sure the transmitter is working properly. I'll be on the other end of the cable.'

*

Getting the transmitter to school had been a bit of a problem. It was too heavy to carry over long distances, and it took up a seat on the bus. Luckily, it fitted into the cool-bag Bright's mum used to do the frozen-food shopping. Bright told everybody who asked that the bag contained samples of anthrax, mad cow disease and bubonic plague. To everyone who knew Bright, this seemed plausible enough, and the bag was left alone. John carried the camera in his sports bag.

The moment the bell went for breaktime, Bright hefted up the cool-bag and he and John shoved through the crowded corridor in pursuit of Mick. After several near-accidents and shin scrapings, they saw Mick disappearing into the boys' toilets.

'Follow that man!'

John stopped dead in his tracks. 'With a video camera?' he exclaimed. 'You must be kidding!'

Bright held out his hands and shrugged. 'What's the problem?'

'If I follow Mick Philips into the toilets with a video camera, he'll think I'm some kind of weirdo! In fact, if I did that, *I'd* think I'm some kind of weirdo!'

Bright had no time to argue the point. At that moment, the door to the toilets opened and Mick walked out. His gaze took in John, Bright, and the camera.

'Are you following me?' he asked.

'Yes (no), er (er) ... no (yes)' said John (and Bright) together.

Mick glared at the pair. 'I hope you aren't, cos if you are ...' He left the threat hanging in the air and stomped off.

Bright groaned. 'That's torn it,' he said.

'Hang on a minute,' said John. 'Why are we chasing Mick all over the school?'

Bright gave an impatient grunt. 'Because we need to capture him on video when he chats Vicky Savage up outside the art room.' There was a pause, as realization suddenly struck Bright. 'Ahh!'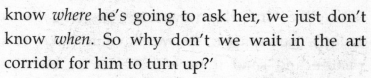

John nodded. 'Exactly – outside the art room. We know *where* he's going to ask her, we just don't know *when*. So why don't we wait in the art corridor for him to turn up?'

Bright's despair had turned into glee. 'He's in the same lessons as us, and he goes home for lunch, so the only time he can ask her out is after school. Good thinking!'

John grinned. 'Sometimes I can be quite bright, Bright.'

Bright scowled.

By the time the bell went for the end of the school day, Bright and John (who had both managed to get out of the final few minutes of the last lesson by claiming that they had to see their form tutor) were set up in prime position.

Bright had decided on different tactics for the filming. He'd set up the transmitter round the corner, out of sight. John was also out of sight, hiding in a store cupboard. Through the half-open door, he had a perfect view of the corridor and the art room. He and Bright had already tested the camera by taking a picture of that day's newspaper.

'We have to do this,' Bright had explained, 'since the first thing we saw yesterday was today's newspaper, so we have to take this picture and send it back to yesterday because we've already done it, or rather we already will have done it.'

John closed his eyes wearily. 'I was with you right up to when you said, "because".'

Now, jammed against paint pots and reams of sugar paper, John waited with growing anticipation. Moments after the bell went, footsteps echoed down the corridor. Here we go, thought John. He poked the camera lens through the gap in the doorway and waited for Vicky to appear.

The cupboard door was wrenched open. Mr Henslowe, clutching an armful of papier-mâché Roman helmets, eyed John suspiciously.

'What're you doing, dear boy?'

'Er – learning my lines, sir,' blurted John unconvincingly.

Mr Henslowe regarded him with astonishment. 'With a camera? In a cupboard? In the dark?' He shook himself. 'Well, no doubt you have your reasons.' He reached above John's head for a paint pot as John writhed with guilt and embarrassment.

Mr Henslowe bustled off. John breathed a sigh of relief and settled down to wait.

To his relief, Vicky Savage appeared a few seconds later. She meandered along the corridor before stopping outside the art room. Then she threw her bag down, leaned against the wall in an I-am-terribly-bored pose and began chewing gum.

Almost simultaneously, Terry McBride and his mates turned into the corridor, talking and giggling. They saw Vicky and stopped dead in their tracks. A hurried whispering followed. Vicky looked up and gave them a cursory glance before returning to the important task of chewing her gum in an I-am-still-terribly-bored manner. Terry nodded towards Vicky and a figure was pushed forward. It was Mick.

John started the camera. Around the corner, Bright grinned as the input signal light came on. The transmitter was getting the camera signal and already sending it on its strange journey to yesterday.

Mick flicked his hair back and walked hesitantly towards Vicky. 'Hello.'

'Goodbye.' Vicky looked away.

Terry and his mates sniggered.

Mick decided it was time for a charm offensive. He reached into his school bag. He pulled out a can, opened it and took a nervous slurp. He gave Vicky a sickly grin.

'Fancy a swig of my Totally Tropical?' he leered.

Vicky turned and eyed Mick up and down. She raised an eyebrow, said nothing and carried on chewing her gum.

Round the corner, Bright could hear every word. It was going exactly as he'd seen yesterday. He smiled at the thought of what was coming next.

Mick looked back towards Terry and the gang. They urged him on with encouraging gestures.

'So ... er ... what are you doing tonight?'

Vicky stared at Mick in stunned disbelief. Was this little Year-Eight creep really trying to chat her up? She stopped chewing her gum and gave Mick a gorgon stare of loathing, disdain and contempt.

At that moment, inside the store cupboard, John leaned forward to get a better shot of what was about to happen. Unfortunately, he caught his leg against a box of poster paints. Several pots fell to the floor with a clatter.

Vicky shot a glance at the cupboard. In the camera viewfinder, John saw her eyes widen, then narrow. Her look of fury sent an icy chill through John's bones.

So, all in all, it probably wasn't the best time for Mick to say, 'Listen, I think you're a real knockout.'

'You're right!' agreed Vicky. She took aim, swung her arm and hit Mick smack on the jaw.

Everyone in the corridor (except Vicky) winced as Mick fell pole-axed to the floor.

But Vicky wasn't done. She picked up Mick's glugging drinks can and tipped the remainder of its sticky contents all over his twitching body.

Then she headed purposefully down the corridor. Terry and his mates scattered. As she passed the cupboard where John was hiding, Vicky gave the door a vicious kick. It slammed shut, sending the camera viewfinder slamming into John's eye. Ignoring the muffled yelp from the cupboard, Vicky stormed out.

Safely hidden around the corner, Bright switched the transmitter off and gave a gleeful chuckle.

'That's a wrap,' he said.

Later that evening, John and Bright sat in the lab and chewed over the day's events.

'But how can you be sure that Mick would have asked Vicky out if you hadn't said anything?' John winced as he pressed a pack of frozen peas against his injured eye.

'Because we saw the future,' insisted Bright. 'And you can't change the future.'

John shook his head as he half remembered one of Mr Henslowe's drama lessons. 'But what about cause and effect?'

Bright looked quizzically at him.

'Like in plays and books and films,' John tried to explain. 'Something happens because something causes it to happen.'

Bright still looked quizzical.

John blundered on. 'If you hadn't said to Mick that he shouldn't ask Vicky out, he'd never have asked her out, so she wouldn't have smacked him and we wouldn't have filmed her smacking him and sent the picture back in time so we could see he was going to get smacked and warn him; but because you warned him, he asked her out and she smacked him, but that wouldn't have happened if you hadn't warned him in the first place ...' Having totally confused himself, John shook his head. 'Anyway,' he went on, 'I'm pretty sure she knew we were filming her.'

'We had to film her,' Bright pointed out

reasonably, 'because that's what we saw yesterday. That's how we knew what she was going to do.'

'Yes, but ...' John tried desperately to marshal his thoughts. 'But would she have smacked Mick if she hadn't known we were filming her?'

'Stop being negative,' said Bright. 'It happened because it happened! There's no doubt that my machine ...'

'*Our* machine.'

'... works. We saw the future.'

'Only because ...'

'Don't start that again,' interrupted Bright. 'Look, we can help people. If we know what's going to happen we can let them know what's going to happen before it happens.'

John's brow furrowed. 'Maybe they won't want to know.'

'Of course they will. Thousands of people look at horoscopes every day. People want to know the future.'

John wasn't convinced.

'OK,' said Bright. 'Tomorrow, I won't tell anybody what's going to happen. We'll just record it tonight and then we'll see if it all comes true or not. All right?'

Not giving John a chance to protest further, Bright reached down towards the recorder and switched it on. A picture began to form.

Bright leaned forward with an eager glint in his eyes. After a few moments, he began to chortle softly to himself.

'Oh dear, oh dear, oh dear,' he said.

CHAPTER SEVEN

'I tell you, it's not a trick! I really can see into the future!'

Bright glared at the circle of hostile, sceptical faces. John hovered around the outside of the circle, looking worried.

If Bright had hoped that the Mick Philips incident would have established his reputation as a prophet, he was mistaken. Mick himself was convinced that Bright had set him up.

'I tell you I didn't put Vicky Savage up to it,' protested Bright. 'I've never even spoken to her. Why should I bother to set you up anyway?'

Mick, unable to think of a convincing reason, shrugged angrily.

'Just to prove how clever you are,' said Meena Patel bitingly. 'You're always doing it.'

Bright gave her a scornful look. 'Why would I want to prove how clever I am?' he drawled with maddening self-assurance. 'Surely it's obvious?'

For several seconds, he was shouted down by a chorus of rude noises and cat-calls.

Nettled, Bright sprang to his feet. 'All right! I'll prove I can see into the future.' He reached into his school bag, and turned to Terry McBride. 'Here's a video disc. I recorded it yesterday afternoon – you'll see the time on the screen when you replay it.'

Terry regarded the box curiously. 'So?'

'It shows several interesting things,' Bright told him. He turned on his heel and pointed at Simon West. 'It shows that something very nasty is going to happen to you this lunchtime …'

Simon's protests were drowned out by a chorus of disbelieving jeers. Bright switched his pointing finger to Meena.

'And it shows what happens when you take your Physics test.' Amid more jeers, Bright folded his arms triumphantly. John groaned. Diplomacy just wasn't Bright's strong point.

Meena looked daggers at Bright. 'Are you saying I'm going to fail it?' she demanded in icy tones.

Bright glanced at John. 'I couldn't possibly say,' he said loftily.

Meena folded her arms. 'As a matter of interest, Mister So-called Clever-clogs, I have no intention of failing that test. I may not be as clever as some people, but I've revised very hard and I am not going to fail, no way!'

'Go, Meena!' yelled Mick.

'And I can look after myself, thanks,' said Simon.

Bright gave them a wolfish smile. 'We'll see. The facts are right there on that disk.' Ignoring John's frantic signs for him to shut up, Bright set his face into the most irritating sneer he could manage and said, 'I'm willing to bet all of you any money you like that what I've recorded on this disc will happen before four o'clock today. Any takers?'

He sat down to uproar.

Terry motioned for silence. 'OK, Bright,' he

said when the din had died down. 'You gave me the disk, so I'll be referee.'

Someone produced a sticky label. With great ceremony, Terry and Bright both signed it before Terry stuck it carefully across the lid of the disk box.

'Sorted,' he said with satisfaction. 'This disk stays in my bag until four o'clock, and if anyone tries to open it, they'll have to break the seal. Fair enough?' He looked round. Several people nodded.

'All right then. At four o'clock we meet in the library to watch the disk. I'll tell Miss Hardy it's for a project. Then, if Bright's wrong, he has to pay us all whatever we've bet him. And if Bright's right,' (there was a chorus of sniggers) 'and he really *can* look into the future, we have to pay him.'

'Have your money ready,' Bright told them with supreme confidence.

Fifteen minutes into the lunch break, Bright was crouched behind the bike shelter making last-minute adjustments to the transmitter while John stood holding the camera and wishing he was somewhere else.

'I don't like this,' he muttered.

'You know what's going to happen,' Bright pointed out. 'All you have to do is point the camera.'

'We ought to warn Simon.'

'Why?' Bright asked without interest.

'Well, you know what's going to happen to him ...'

Bright gave a long-suffering sigh. 'Whether we warned him or not, it would still happen. We know that because we've seen it. It's inevitable, so what's the point?' His face became hard. 'In any case, it's about time those idiots in our class were taught a lesson.'

John shook his head. There was simply no point in arguing. Anyway, maybe Bright was right. Maybe once they'd seen something on the Faster-than-light Show, it really would happen, no matter what.

There was a distant tinkle of bells playing a rather twitchy version of 'Greensleeves'.

'Here we go,' said Bright. An unpleasant grin spread over his face. 'Lights, camera, action!'

Glumly, John stepped out from the bike shelter and pointed the camera at the school gates.

A battered, but gaudily painted, ice-cream van exploded on to the street like the contents of a party popper. It rolled up outside the school gates and stopped in a haze of blue exhaust fumes. The tuneless jingle switched off in mid-bong.

Kids stampeded out to be first in line for a Mister Licky.

Simon and a gang of his mates lounged against the school gates.

The first kid peeled away from the queue with a Mister Licky Supreme (giant-sized cone, two flakes, nuts and raspberry-flavoured topping) in his hand. Eyes half closed in ice-cream ecstasy, he took a lingering lick at his purchase.

Simon nudged a couple of his mates. They strolled towards the kid with the gigantic ice cream. As they wandered past, Simon's hand shot out and snatched the cone from the kid's grasp.

"'Ere, that's mine!' piped the kid.

'*Was* yours,' Simon corrected. His mates guffawed.

Bright watched the developing situation with ghoulish glee. 'Now for the good bit,' he crowed.

'Giz it back,' whined the kid.

'Sure,' leered Simon. 'If you can reach it.' He held the ice cream above his head and waved it about. His mates haw-hawed and high-fived at the little kid's ineffectual attempts to jump high enough to recover his ice cream.

'Is there a problem?'

The words were spoken in a bass rumble. Simon turned slowly as a gigantic form standing behind him blotted out the sun. He looked up ... and up ...

His laughter faded.

'Why have you taken my brother's ice cream?'

'Oh. Hello, Crusher,' Simon quavered. He looked around for support. His mates had vanished.

Crusher Wilson was captain of the school rugby team, when he wasn't kick-boxing or weight-training.

'Is this your brother then?' squeaked Simon. Crusher nodded slowly. 'Yeah, well – I was just looking after his ice cream.' Simon thrust it at the kid. 'Here y'are,' he said with ghastly joviality.

Crusher's brother folded his arms. 'Don't want it after you've had it!'

A gorilla-like hand took Simon's arm in an iron grip.

'You like ice cream, do you?' Crusher's voice was like distant thunder.

He led the trembling Simon towards the ice cream van. The queue parted to let him through.

'Four Giant Mister Lickys please.' Crusher ignored Simon's struggles as the grinning ice-cream man placed four enormous cones in the holder at the front of the counter.

'Here you are then,' growled Crusher. 'Enjoy.'

He took one of the gigantic cones and, with

slow deliberation, shoved it into Simon's mouth. Simon's squeals of protest were instantly muffled.

A crowd of kids watched entranced as Crusher took the second and third cones. Holding them either side of Simon's head, he rammed one into each of his ears. There was a burst of applause.

He then picked up the fourth cone, turned it upside down, and stuck it on top of Simon's head. It sat there like a very small and messy dunce's cap. The crowd clapped and cheered.

Crusher turned to his audience. 'Thank you. And for my final trick ...' Ignoring the mute appeal in his victim's eyes, Crusher reached down and stretched out the waistband of Simon's trousers. He nodded at his brother's ice cream, which was now beginning to melt in Simon's trembling hand. 'You know what to do.'

With a stifled moan, Simon held the ice cream over the kangaroo-pouch of his trousers. He closed his eyes. He gulped. He let the ice cream drop.

Crusher released his grip. Simon's trousers snapped back. John, watching through the viewfinder, sucked in a sharp breath in sympathy.

Dripping ice cream, Simon shuffled away in a penguin-waddle.

'Where are you goin'?' Crusher's arm shot out. He grabbed Simon by the scruff. 'You haven't paid for those ice creams you've had yet.'

Simon groaned. Reaching into his sticky trousers, he turned to the ice-cream man and pulled out a handful of coins.

Crusher pulled one of the cones away from Simon's ear. 'That's a good boy,' he rumbled. 'And don't forget the one you owe my brother.'

John switched the camera off. He turned round and saw the look on Bright's face.

'You're gloating,' he said accusingly.

Bright hastily wiped the grin off his face. 'I'm not. Come on, help me shift this stuff. We need to get it to the science lab before the next period.'

Seething with silent resentment, John complied.

There was silence in the library as the picture on the screen faded to black.

'It's a fix,' Mick said hoarsely. 'You filmed all that today.'

Bright regarded the speaker scornfully. Terry shook his head.

'No,' he said firmly. 'I kept that disk in my bag all day. I never left it anywhere, and no one came near it. Anyway, the seal wasn't broken. You all saw that.'

There were reluctant nods at this.

'I still say he switched disks on you,' Mick insisted.

'He didn't.' Terry looked around. 'He couldn't have. I'm the referee and I say Bright has won.' He reached into his pocket. 'It's pay-up time.'

Reluctantly, people handed over cash and IOUs while Bright beamed. 'Look on it as a small fee for a glimpse into the future,' he said. His grin widened. 'I suppose you could call it Pay As You Déjà-vu.'

There was a sound of sobbing from the back of the room. Heads turned. Meena was sitting with her face buried in her hands. Her shoulders were shaking.

'Aww, Meena, what is it?' Another girl put an arm round Meena's shoulders. 'What's the matter?'

'I really – *sniff* – worked hard for – *sniff* – that

test, but when – *sniff* – Mr Allen said we had to revise – *sniff* – electrolytes, I thought – *sniff* – he said electric lights and I – *sniff* – revised the wrong topic and – *sniff* – I failed it and now – *sniff* – I'll have to do the repeat – *sniff* – test and I – *sniff* – had tickets to see – *sniff* – my favourite band at the – *sniff* – Arena, but now my mum will say I've got to do my revision instead and – *sniff* – she won't let me go ...' Meena broke into a renewed fit of sobbing.

Everyone turned to Bright with looks of deep disgust.

'Hang on a minute,' Bright protested as his classmates turned their backs on him and began to file out, 'it's not my fault ...'

As the last of their classmates left the room in pointed silence, Bright turned to John in bewilderment. 'What's got into them?'

'You have!' John had had enough. 'You make me sick. You don't care about anyone else's feelings at all, do you? Just so long as you can prove that you're right, you don't care who gets hurt.'

'That's not fair!' Bright jumped up in a fury. 'I didn't tell Meena what to revise and I didn't tell her she was going to fail.'

'You made it pretty obvious. As soon as she realized she'd revised the wrong unit, she *knew* she'd failed. If you hadn't said anything, maybe she'd have remembered enough stuff about electrolytes to get a pass mark.' John pointed an accusing finger at Bright. 'If people know what's going to happen to them, the effect becomes part of the cause!'

Bright looked uneasy. 'All right, don't go on,' he muttered, 'nobody died ...'

The screen flickered once more. A picture began to form.

Startled, John checked the DVD player. 'It's still playing back.'

Bright gave the screen a surprised look. 'I thought that was the end of the recording.'

'So did I, but there must have been something else that came on later.' John sat down beside Bright. Together, they watched the screen.

After a while, their eyes grew round with horror.

'Scholes! Scholes!' Bright charged into the hall where lights were being rigged for *Julius Caesar.*

The sixth-former looked round irritably. 'Oh,

it's you,' he said in a less-than-friendly way. 'What do you want?'

'To warn you!' Bright looked up briefly as John staggered into the hall in his wake, groaning under the weight of the camera and transmitter.

Scholes gave an impatient grunt and went back to his task of fitting a red-coloured filter into a theatre light. 'Warn me about what?'

Bright grabbed Scholes by the shoulder. He pointed to the A-frame ladder set up in the middle of the hall. 'Don't go up there.'

Scholes stared at him. 'Is that all?' he asked. 'And then these lanterns will just hang themselves, will they?'

Bright shook his head urgently. 'I'm warning you ...'

Scholes grabbed Bright's shirt front. 'And I'm warning you. Stay out of my way.' He released Bright. 'You're really pathetic, do you know that? You just can't stand the idea that you're not allowed to do the lighting, so you try to mess it up for everyone else. Just push off.'

Brushing aside Bright's protests, Scholes picked up the lantern and started to climb the ladder. With his heart in his mouth, John automatically switched the camera on and started to film.

Scholes was nearly at the top of the ladder when his foot came down on the plug dangling from the lantern's power cable. His foot slipped off the rung. With a despairing cry, he plunged to the ground.

Bright gazed in horror at the moaning figure.

Scholes's leg was bent underneath him at a strange angle.

'It wasn't my fault,' Bright whispered. 'I tried to warn him.' He turned a beseeching look on John. 'Didn't I? Didn't I try to warn him?'

John gave him back look for look. 'And if you hadn't – if you hadn't made him angry – would he still have fallen then?'

John raced away to fetch help. Bright tore his gaze away from Scholes's broken leg and closed his eyes.

CHAPTER EIGHT

Another Big Bang

Scholes's unlucky break was a lucky break for Bright. As he said to John, it just went to show that even though the idea was scientifically inaccurate, every cloud really did have a silver lining. Bright was the only student at Elmley with the skills to do the lighting for *Julius Caesar*. And because there was no time to train anyone else, Mr Henslowe had to talk to the Head in order to try and persuade him to let Bright back near the lighting box. It was a very long discussion.

Eventually the meeting finished and Mr Henslowe caught up with Bright and John in the corridor at breaktime.

'I trust your extraordinary method of learning lines has paid off,' he asked John.

John nodded guiltily.

'Good.' He turned to Bright. 'Now, dear boy, I have prevailed upon the Head to reverse his ban on you concerning lighting and so forth.'

Bright's eyes lit up. 'Oh good, I can work on those ideas that I had,' he enthused.

'You will not!' boomed Mr Henslowe. 'I have been informed by the Head that I am totally responsible for you and your behaviour! I have had to swear a blood oath that nothing will go wrong! And nothing will! You will stick exactly to Scholes's lighting plan! And if you so much as alter one jot of it ...' Mr Henslowe paused for dramatic effect, 'I will do to you what Titus Andronicus did to the sons of Tamora, Queen of the Goths.'

Bright wasn't sure who Titus Andronicus was. 'What did he do, sir?'

'He had them brutally murdered, baked them into pies, and fed them to their own mother!'

'Ah,' said Bright. 'I suppose I could stick to Scholes's plan.'

'Could?!' bawled Mr Henslowe. 'Could?! You *will*!'

Scholes's misfortune added to the general uneasiness created by Bright and the Faster-than-light Show. Lots of people were giving Bright a wide berth and shying away from knowing what was going to happen to them. Even Terry McBride had been wary about Bright's ability to record the future.

'If you'd lived in the Middle Ages, you'd have been burnt as a witch,' he told Bright.

'Witches were female,' Bright retorted. 'I'm male. I'd have been a wizard.'

'Whatever; you'd still have been burnt. And serve you right,' added Terry maliciously.

Bright gave Terry a superior look. 'I'd be very careful what you say, Terry. People who make fun of things they don't understand usually come to a sticky end ...'

Terry turned pale. 'Why? What have you seen?' he demanded in a shaking voice.

'Oh, nothing,' said Bright deliberately. 'Just a general observation. Now if you'll excuse me, I've got to sort out some lighting.'

'You shouldn't have wound Terry up like that,' said John.

'He asked for it,' replied Bright matter-of-factly.

'But you haven't seen anything bad that happens to him,' John pointed out. There was a pause. 'Have you?' he added.

'No. Not yet.' Bright smiled gleefully. 'Anyway, I thought that you were against looking into the future.'

John grimaced. He had to admit, there was something addictive about seeing into the future, which was why he was back in Bright's lab for another edition of the Faster-than-light Show.

Bright pointed to a blinking light on the DVD recorder. 'Something must have come in yesterday while I was out,' he said. He flicked the playback switch. 'Let's see what the future holds for some poor soul.'

The monitor flickered. A familiar location appeared on the screen.

'It's Dodgy Dave's!' cried John.

'I wonder why we're filming his warehouse?' pondered Bright. 'Do you think that ...'

KABOOM!

Bright and John stared in horror at the screen. One minute Dave's warehouse was there, then in the blinking of an eye, it turned into a roaring ball of flame as a tremendous explosion ripped through the building. The picture on the monitor shook and the sky was lit up by trails of fire.

'That must be all the ammo going off!' exclaimed Bright.

There was one more terrific bang and then the picture was lost. Static lines filled the screen and the speakers blasted out white noise.

Bright and John looked in horror at each other.

'When's it going to happen?' squeaked John.

Bright checked the time on the recording. 'In about an hour,' he gulped.

'We've got to warn him!' John cried. He sprinted for the lab door.

'Don't forget the camera and the transmitter,' yelled Bright.

John spun round to face him. 'Are you some kind of ghoul? Dave might be in there! Are you saying we just stand there filming while he gets blown to smithereens?'

'We've got to film it,' Bright said reasonably. 'We've seen it on the monitor, so we had to be there to film it. Or put another way, we've got to be there to film it, otherwise we can't have seen it.'

John clenched his fists. 'Forget the filming. Come on!'

'We can't,' Bright told him. 'Do you know what would happen if we didn't film something we've already seen?'

'No!'

'Neither do I,' admitted Bright, 'but it could be catastrophic. We'd be creating a paradox.'

'A parawhat?'

'In this reality,' said Bright, 'we film Dave's warehouse blowing up. We know that because we've just seen the film. If we don't film it, we could be catapulted into a whole different reality. The universe as we know it might cease to exist.'

John gulped. Alternative realities and parallel universes were always cropping up in the science-fiction stories he read. They always seemed to be inhabited by giant killer robots or insects the size of dinosaurs.

'All right!' he snapped. He clattered back down the stairs and snatched the camera and transmitter. 'Now come on!'

As they skidded into Dave's yard, Bright and John were relieved to see that the warehouse was still in one piece.

'Phew, we're in time.' John breathed a sigh of relief.

They found Dave in his office.

Breathlessly, and interrupting each other every few seconds, Bright and John told Dave what they'd seen on the Faster-than-light Show.

At first, Dave was inclined to be sceptical.

'Hold on a cotton pickin' minute,' he growled. 'You're tellin' me you got some cockamamie machine that can look into the future?'

'That's right.'

'That's pretty weird, even for you, Vernie.'

John was hopping about with anxiety. 'Look, we did see it, you've got to believe us! It's going to happen.' He looked at his watch and gulped. 'Very soon!'

'You're crazy! There ain't nothin' explosive in here. It's all bona fide, practically guaranteed ... uh oh.' Dave's face took on a whitish tinge.

Bright pounced on his uncertainty. 'Uh oh what?'

'Waaal,' said Dave hesitantly, 'I just received a shipment of mines from a very special source.'

'Where from?' asked Bright.

'There's need to know, boys, and there's don't need to know, and you fit squarely into that last category.' Dave drummed his fingers on the desk. 'Maybe they didn't remove all the explosive charges. Damn Russkies ...' He clapped a hand to his mouth. 'I never said that.'

Bright shook his head. 'I never heard it.'

'I'd better go check.' Dave rammed his hat on

110

his head and reached into his shirt pocket. He selected a small black cigar from a battered packet, and clamped it between his teeth.

'You dudes had better wait outside. This could be dangerous.'

John groaned. 'There's no time!' He tapped his watch. 'You don't want to be in here when it blows up!'

Dave stared at him. 'I don't want it to blow up, period.' He squared his shoulders and chewed on the cigar. 'Like I told ma buddy, Big John Wayne, "A man's gotta do what a man's gotta do," and that's all there is to it, boys. Now get the heck outta here.'

Although it wasn't cold outside the warehouse, John still shivered. 'Do you think Dave'll manage to sort it out?' he asked Bright.

'Maybe. You know what he's like.'

'I do. That's the problem,' said John ruefully.

'I'm sure he'll be all right,' Bright reassured John. He swung the camera on to his shoulder and pointed towards the warehouse. 'We may as well make sure the universe will still be here tomorrow …'

Inside the warehouse, Dave unscrewed the cover on the first mine. He paused to wipe his palms, which were damp with sweat. With a great effort, he controlled his shaking hands and lifted off the cover plate.

Empty! There was no explosive charge. Dave heaved a sigh of relief and moved on to the second mine.

Outside, Bright lifted his head and sniffed at the air. John looked quizzically at him. 'What's the matter?'

'Can you smell anything?' queried Bright.

Dave finished checking the second mine. He mopped his brow. This was ticklish work. A man could sure use a smoke at a time like this ...

Dave bit hard on his cigar and reached for his lighter ...

John sniffed. 'There is something,' he agreed. 'It smells like ...

He stared at Bright in horror.

'Gas?'

KAAAABBBBBBOOM!!!!!

The two boys were knocked backwards by the force of the blast. As they shielded their eyes a series of explosions lit up the sky in a repetition of the display they had seen on the screen earlier. Debris began whistling past them. Bright dropped the camera and hit the deck as something hot and dangerous whizzed by his head. John decided that it was time to play follow-my-leader and dived on to the floor next to Bright.

Eventually the explosions petered out. John looked up. Tears began to form in his eyes. Bright felt a lump in his throat. The two boys picked themselves up off the floor and stared at the blackened shell of Dave's warehouse.

John looked at Bright for some kind of reassurance. 'Do you think …?'

Bright shook his head mournfully.

'Sweet jumpin' Jesaphiah!' A blackened figure staggered out of the warehouse.

'Dave!' yelled John joyfully.

Smoke drifted from Dave's singed clothes and his moustache seemed to be smouldering. 'Whoah, boys. I've not had that feelin' since I ate a chilli vindaloo.' Following the boys' awestruck glances, he turned and surveyed the blackened shell of the warehouse. 'Ma business! A goner!' he moaned.

John's relief at seeing Dave alive changed into

anger. He turned on Bright. 'It's all your fault! If we hadn't come here and warned Dave, he wouldn't have gone looking for the mine.'

'We had to film it because we already had!' Bright retorted. 'We'd already seen the future and you can't change it!'

The two boys continued in a series of recriminations that might have ended in blows if Dave hadn't interrupted the argument.

'Hold on to those wild mustangs for just one cotton pickin' moment,' he said. 'You can see into the future, right?'

John nodded eagerly. 'Yes, we've discovered Vernons, they're …'

'Whoah, pardner, N to K! Don't blind me with the technology.' He turned and looked Bright straight in the eye. 'All I need to know is, are you Mr Crystal Ball?'

'I suppose so,' said Bright, nodding.

Dave began to laugh. 'Oh boy, are we in the cabbage!'

There was a pause as Bright and John looked at each other.

'Yes, boys, we are in the lettuce!'

'Why is he talking about vegetables?' John

hissed to Bright. 'Do you think the blast has made him go a bit funny?'

'No more than usual, I suspect,' replied Bright. 'What are you talking about, Dave?'

Dave began to hop about. 'Boys, we are in the gravy and the land of the long green! We are gonna see more spondulicks, greenbacks, wads, moolah, dibs, billies and beans than we'll know what to do with!'

John and Bright still looked puzzled.

Without warning, Dave burst into song. 'Who's gonna be a millionaire? I am!'

'I don't believe this!' cried Bright. 'Your business has just gone up in smoke and you're happy. Why?'

'Vernie, boy,' drawled Dave, 'if you know the future, you know what the gee-gees are going to do.'

'The what?'

'Horses,' explained Dave. 'We'll know which horse is going to win. Not only that, we'll know the results of football matches, how the stock market is doing and best of all – the National Lottery. We'll know which numbers are going to be drawn, so we can buy the winning ticket!'

Realization dawned on Bright and John.

Dave waved a dismissive hand at the smoking warehouse. 'Forget about this little problem here. We're gonna be seriously rich!'

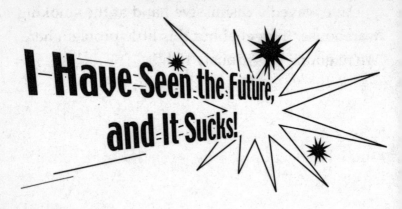

CHAPTER NINE

I Have Seen the Future, and It Sucks!

'It's cheating!' said John, scowling at Bright's back.

Bright brushed off John's protests. 'You can't change the future,' he reiterated. 'And the future is Bright!'

'But the Lottery is supposed to be a game of chance.'

'Somebody's got to win it.'

'Exactly!' yelled John triumphantly. 'And if you go and choose the winning numbers because your machine can look into the future, then *somebody* isn't going to win it, are they? Because *you're* going to win it instead. By cheating!' He folded his arms in triumph.

Bright gave him an irritated glare. 'Look, I'm trying to reset the power levels so that we can see as far into the future as possible. If I make one mistake, the transmitter won't work. So shut up and let me get on with it.' He went back to work. 'Anyway, we owe it to Dave ...'

'No, *we* don't!' John shook his head angrily. 'Leave me out of this.'

'All right.' Bright turned to him in exasperation. 'Do I take it from your attitude, Mister Squeaky-clean, that you don't want to go shares on the winning ticket?'

John's eyes bulged. 'Ah, well, I didn't exactly say that ...'

'Aha!' Bright dived back into the inner workings of the transmitter.

'That's not fair!' protested John. 'If I don't take a share, it means you and Dave get to share everything and I don't get anything. If we don't do it at all, then *none* of us gets anything.'

'So when it comes right down to it, you're not a goody two-shoes at all, you're just a spoil-sport.' Bright gave John a particularly nasty glance. 'Now go away and stop bothering me.'

John was trembling with righteous indignation. 'All right! I'm going. And since you ask, no, I don't want a share of the winning ticket. You and Dave can have the lot, and I hope it chokes you!' John stormed out of the house.

Bright flung the screwdriver to the floor and raced out after him. 'Go on then, get lost!' he yelled at John's retreating back. 'Don't come crying to me tomorrow asking for your share back, OK? And it's not cheating. Can I help it if I'm brilliant?'

'Hey, Vernie!'

Bright had been so busy yelling at John he'd not heard the sound of an approaching engine. Turning, he gaped as a long, low, rakish convertible slid smoothly to the kerb beside him.

The car had about an acre of metallic pink paintwork streaked with gleaming chrome. The radiator grille was set in a shark's tooth grin, an effect that was reinforced by huge fins that swept back towards the rear.

Sitting in the driver's seat, wearing a revolting

Hawaiian shirt and a big grin, was Dodgy Dave.

'Hi there, amigo,' he said. He patted the car door. 'Get a load of the wheels. Smooth with a capital Smoo, huh? You like?'

Bright gawped at the vast vehicle. 'What is it?' he asked sourly, 'A boat?'

Dave snorted. 'This, my friend, is a 1959 Cadillac Series 62 Convertible, V8 engine, fully restored and, as of ten minutes ago, the property of yours truly.'

'You mean you've bought that thing?' gasped Bright in disbelief.

Dave grinned at him. 'Hey, Vernie-baby, if you've got it, flaunt it.'

'You haven't got it yet,' Bright pointed out.

'Details, my man, details. I took out a small loan with Big Al.'

Bright stared at him. 'Big Al? The loan shark?'

'He's a good ol' boy.'

'He's a psychopath. He sleeps in a coffin. He eats raw liver. He wears a barbed-wire singlet.'

'You worry too much.' Dave pointed at John, who was just turning the corner at the end of Bright's street. 'What's eatin' your buddy?'

Bright gave Dave a rundown on John's

objections to the Lottery scheme as Dave, with many a backward glance at his new toy, followed him into the house.

Dave shrugged. 'Hey, if he wants to wimp out, it's his problem. Who needs him?'

'Right,' said Bright without conviction. He pointed at the transmitter sitting on a coffee table on the opposite side of the TV to the recorder. 'I've connected the transmitter to the TV instead of the camera. On Saturday night when the Lottery show comes on, all we have to do is transmit the pictures into the past. Of course, before that I'll have connected the TV back to the recorder and played the recording in time to buy the ticket.'

Dave's eyes were glazed. 'Whatever.' Then he eyed the transmitter and rubbed his hands together. 'So, this is the piece of hardware that's going to make our fortunes?'

'If I ever get to finish the adjustments I'm *trying* to make!' Bright snapped.

'Don't let me stop you.' Dave watched as Bright picked up his screwdriver and prodded carefully at the machine's circuits. 'Pretend I'm not here. Don't pay me no never-mind. I'll just kind of merge into the background. You just carry on like I wasn't ...'

'Will you shut up? How can I think with you gabbling on?' Seething with irritation, Bright gave the transmitter a final hurried tweak. He replaced the cover and pressed the POWER switch. 'Bingo,' he muttered as the lights came on and settled to a steady glow. He turned the TV on. 'It'll take a minute to warm up,' he told Dave. 'I'd better check all the connections.'

'Sure.' Dave had grown fidgety. 'Hey, come an' eyeball the Caddy while you're waitin'. Whaddayasay?'

Ignoring Bright's protests, Dave hauled him outside to admire the monstrous car. A picture appeared on the TV screen. The applause of a studio audience burst from the speaker.

By the time Bright managed to get rid of Dave, fifteen minutes later, the TV was showing the News. Satisfied that the set-up was working, Bright switched it off.

Next day at school, John wouldn't talk to Bright, or even look at him.

After a few failed attempts to start a

conversation, Bright gave up and ignored John as pointedly as John was ignoring him. Bright told himself that John was being stupid. John was dead lucky that a genius like Bright had ever agreed to be his friend in the first place, and if John wanted to be ungrateful and childish, why should Bright care? Nevertheless, by the end of the day, when John stomped off to his *Julius Caesar* rehearsal without a word, Bright felt alone and miserable. He mooched into the backstage area of the hall, looking for something to do.

All the lights were in position and all the lighting scenes were programmed into the computer-controlled lighting board. There really wasn't anything left for Bright to do. Then he spotted the corpse of Julius Caesar, a carefully made and very lifelike dummy. It was to be used for the funeral scene in which Mark Antony does his famous *'Friends, Romans, countrymen ...!'* speech. Bright eyed the corpse with interest, then calculation, and finally with gloating satisfaction. He had an idea. He'd show John. He'd show all of them!

'Aha!' he said softly to himself.

*

The morning sun, streaming through a gap in the curtains, woke Bright. Blearily, he turned over, and blinked at his alarm clock.

The time on the clock read 7.30. That was OK, the receiver would be picking up the pictures from the Lottery and the DVD would be recording them. He could look at them later. It was a good job he'd remembered to set the DVD up last night.

He had remembered, hadn't he?

For about ten seconds, Bright told himself not to be so stupid. Then he flung himself out of bed and pelted down to the cellar.

He gave a strangled cry of horror. The receiver and DVD recorder were turned off. He might already have missed the draw! With a whimper of panic, Bright hit the POWER button on the receiver and the DVD recorder and groped for the pencil and pad he had left ready the night before.

He held his breath as the TV warmed up. His estimate that his machine could look thirty-six hours into the future was a bit hit-and-miss – he could be out by an hour or more either way. The Lottery draw happened on Saturday evening, so the winning numbers should be coming in on the

Faster-than-light Show at about breakfast time on Friday – which was now!

A picture swam into focus on the monitor screen. Bright sighed with relief: the screen showed numbered balls being whisked round in a drum. The draw was just about to happen. He hadn't missed it! With an unsteady hand, Bright scribbled the winning numbers down on his pad. As soon as the numbers were all drawn and rearranged on the screen in the correct order, Bright switched off the receiver and replayed the recording on the DVD. He checked the numbers twice.

Satisfied, he put the pad in his bag and went back upstairs to get ready for school.

It was impossible for John and Bright to ignore each other completely as they had both been let off classes to rehearse for *Julius Caesar*. They had to be content with speaking to each other as little as possible.

During a break in rehearsals, Bright wandered over, accidentally-on-purpose, to where John was sitting.

'Er – how are rehearsals going?' he asked casually.

'OK,' said John uncomfortably. 'I've – er – learned my lines now. I think.'

'Oh,' said Bright. 'Good. That's good. So we've got the technical rehearsal on Sunday, and the dress rehearsal is on Monday, isn't it?'

'That's right.'

'Right, right.' Bright put his hands in his pockets. 'I – uh – picked up the Lottery draw this morning.'

'Did you?' said John flatly.

'Yes. Dave was going to get the ticket today.' Bright hesitated. 'I don't suppose you …?'

'No.'

'No. OK.' Bright picked up his bag. 'I suppose I'll see you Sunday then.'

'I suppose so.'

'Right. Well, see you.'

'See you.'

By Saturday evening, John was bored to tears.

Then it occurred to him that he would be at rehearsals all day on Sunday, and wouldn't have time to do his homework. He sighed. What a life – having nothing better than homework to do on a Saturday night. Dragging his feet like a condemned man mounting the steps to the scaffold, John fetched his bag from the hall and fished around inside.

He pulled out a book: *Quantum Mechanics Made Difficult*. He stared at it. That surely couldn't be his. He took a closer look at the bag and groaned.

It was Bright's bag. Bright must have picked up John's bag on Friday afternoon, and John had picked up Bright's without noticing. He rummaged in the bag again. Had Bright written down the homework task?

John pulled out a spiral-bound notebook from the bag. He leafed through it.

It was blank, apart from some numbers on the first page. No homework there, then. He'd have to … John paused and looked at the numbers again. They looked like … yes, this was where Bright had written down the winning Lottery numbers.

As he looked at them, John shook himself. He stared in disbelief. 'Oo – er,' he said softly.

There was an urgent knock on the front door.

Bright looked across at Dave, who was sprawled on the sofa shovelling popcorn into his mouth with the single-mindedness of a mechanical digger, his eyes glued to the TV screen. Bright sighed. 'I'll get it,' he said morosely.

He went out into the corridor and opened the front door. John stood on the step holding a school bag in his arms and jiggling from foot to foot.

'Oh!' Bright recovered from his surprise. 'Er – come in.' He stepped back.

'Hey, Vernie!' Dave's voice echoed from the living room, 'git your sorry butt in here! They're just fixin' to start!'

Bright turned apologetically to John. 'I'd better go in,' he said hesitantly, 'we're watching the Lottery show – er, we've got to send it through the transmitter back to yesterday …'

'I know,' said John urgently. 'That's what I've come to tell you about …'

'Hey, home boy!'

With a helpless glance at John, Bright turned and went into the living room. John followed.

Dave gave John an unfriendly glance. 'Oh, it's the washout. Listen, dude, you threw your hand in already. If you've come creeping round here hoping for a cut, forget it.'

John glared at him. 'No, I didn't.' He pulled the notebook out of Bright's bag. 'I came here because …'

'Yehaaah!' Dave whooped as the TV picture changed. 'Here comes the draw. Pipe down, kiddo. Let's have some awed respect for two guys who are about to hit the jackpot.'

John shrugged resignedly and sat down. Bright fumbled his way to a chair. On the screen, the balls spun around. The first ball dropped.

'Thirty-six!' Dave checked a number on his ticket, and kissed it. 'I'm countin' on you, baby,' he crooned. 'Make Poppa proud.'

Another ball dropped. 'Twenty-eight!' said the TV announcer.

Dave stared at his ticket, transfixed with shock. 'Twenty-eight? I ain't got no twenty-eight.' He checked the ticket frantically. 'What gives?'

'Nineteen!'

'Oh, man,' moaned Dave, 'this has got to be a put-on.'

Dave stared at his ticket in stunned silence as the rest of the numbers were called. Not one, bar the first, matched the numbers on his ticket.

Bright switched the TV set off.

'That's what I came round to tell you.' John's voice broke the silence. Bright and Dave turned dumbfounded faces on him.

'Those numbers – we took each other's bag by mistake on Friday, and as soon as I saw those numbers I knew.'

'Knew what?' croaked Bright.

'Those aren't tonight's numbers. They were the numbers from the midweek draw. Last Wednesday.'

Bright's jaw dropped. 'What?'

Suddenly, he leaped up and tore the cover off the transmitter. He glared at the wiring for a moment or two, then he threw his head back and gave a howl of despair.

'The polarity!' he screeched.

John stared at him. 'What?'

'I was connecting all this up on Wednesday night. First you interrupted me …' Bright glared at John. 'Then Dave dragged me off to see his stupid car and, what with everything, I connected the positive to the negative and the negative to the positive, and somehow …'

John finished the sentence. 'The transmitter must have sent Wednesday's draw thirty-six hours into the future, instead of today's draw thirty-six hours into the past.'

Bright gave a moan of frustration. 'I wondered what had happened to the test signal I transmitted on Wednesday night. I wondered why I hadn't already seen it! I hadn't seen it because it wasn't being sent back into the past, it was going the other way!'

Dave turned a stricken face to them. 'I guess this means we don't win.'

'That's exactly what it means.'

The ticket dropped from Dave's nerveless fingers. 'I'm dead,' he moaned. 'Big Al is gonna kill me.'

Bright ran frantic fingers through his hair. 'Never mind!' he said, 'I can fix the machine. We can get the winning numbers for next week.'

Dave shook his head. 'I can't pay Big Al back next week,' he said, 'on account of, people who mess with Big Al don't get no next week.' He made his way to the door. 'I'd like a quiet funeral, something dignified, no flowers by request ...'

The door closed. Bright looked at John.

John shrugged. 'Sorry,' he said. He looked anxiously at the closed door. 'What do you suppose Big Al will do to Dave?'

'I expect Dave will talk his way out of it somehow. He usually does.' Bright turned and glared at the transmitter. 'As for this heap of junk, I'm going to fix it right now.' He pulled a

screwdriver from his pocket and began to poke around.

John's eyes widened as he noticed the lights on the machine. 'Watch out!' he called. 'You've forgotten to switch it ...'

There was a blue flash. Bright was catapulted across the room.

'... off,' John concluded lamely. He rushed over to Bright, who was already groaning and trying to sit up.

'I'm OK,' he muttered. 'I must have ...'

As Bright staggered to his feet, the RECORD light blinked on the recorder.

Bright groaned. 'Now what?'

'Ignore it,' said John.

Bright shook his head woozily. 'It might be something important. We'd better take a look.'

Casting anxious looks at Bright, John switched the TV on and turned it to the video channel. The receiver hummed as it picked up a signal from the future and sent it to the recorder.

The picture cleared. Bright stared at the TV screen. John followed his gaze, and gave a gasp of horror.

The figure on the screen was unmistakably Bright. Only his face was visible: the rest of him was covered with a white sheet. His eyes were closed.

He was lying in a coffin. Candles flickered at each corner. He was surrounded by indistinct figures, whose heads were bowed with sorrow. John was bending over him with tears streaming down his face.

The recorder shut down. The TV picture faded.

Bright turned a stricken face to John. He pointed a trembling finger at the blank screen.

'Did you see that?' he croaked. 'I'm going to die.'

CHAPTER TEN

Prophet and Loss

The technical rehearsal had gone off smoothly.

Throughout the whole of Sunday, Mr Henslowe had been in a pitiable state of nerves. At every lighting change he had seemed to be offering up a silent prayer. All day, he had been casting nervous glances up at the lighting box, waiting for the latest Bright disaster to manifest itself.

He needn't have worried. Bright was listless and hollow-eyed. He had set the video recording system up with minimal fuss and placed the cameras where nobody would trip over them. He had operated the lighting board with absent-minded disinterest. He had missed a few cues but, as far as Mr Henslowe was concerned, that was a small price to pay for a rehearsal in which nothing had blown up or burnt down.

'You're not yourself, dear boy,' he had said to Bright. 'Thank goodness.'

Even John had managed to stumble through his lines with few mistakes. At the end of the rehearsal, he had gone up to the lighting box where Bright was staring hopelessly at the transmitter.

'It seems to be working OK,' he said.

Bright turned a haggard face to John.

'It's working perfectly,' he said tonelessly. 'Since I switched the settings back to normal, it's been working exactly as it should have worked in the first place.' He gave the transmitter a look of pure dread. 'It just won't send pictures back in time any more! When I tried to adjust it last night I caused a short circuit, and that seems to have stopped whatever was causing the faster-than-light effect.'

John sighed. 'Never mind. At least it seems to be doing a good job of videoing the play.'

'Oh, good.' Bright gave a sniff of self-pity. 'I'll

remember that as I suffer whatever hideous death fate has in store for me.'

'Cheer up, it may never happen,' said John encouragingly. 'We may be reading the picture wrong.'

Bright pointed at the screen. 'I was lying in a coffin. I was covered with a white sheet. My eyes were closed. I was surrounded by flowers and candles and people crying their eyes out. I don't think anybody was expecting me to get up in a minute and start doing press-ups!'

'All right, all right. I was just trying to look on the bright side.' John's brain caught up with his mouth. He winced.

'Oh, very funny,' said Bright bitterly. 'Look, there's no good fooling ourselves. We know I'm going to die – we've seen it! We just don't know when. Right now the transmitter isn't sending faster-than-light signals, so it can't send a picture of my death back to yesterday. But if I fix it, it will be able to.'

John pounced on the obvious answer. 'Then don't fix it.'

'But I *must* fix it!' howled Bright. 'I must have – I mean, I must be going to fix it, because we've seen the picture it sent – will send – back, so somehow I'm going to fix it even if I don't want to fix it, and as soon as it's fixed, I could die at any minute!'

'Maybe you won't die at all.'

Bright shook his head hopelessly. 'Everything we've seen happening on this Faster-than-light Show has come true. I've told you a hundred times – you can't change the future.'

By the end of the dress rehearsal on Monday afternoon, Mr Henslowe was positively beaming. True, he'd had to tell the Plebeians off for swapping trading cards during Mark Antony's big speech. Brutus had spilt yoghurt down his toga, and two Roman senators had had a punch-up in the dressing room.

On the other hand, Bright had given hardly a moment's trouble. The lighting had been more or less on cue, and very little of the play had actually taken place in total darkness. Even Bright's unnecessarily elaborate video system appeared to be working to perfection. Mr Henslowe had gone home whistling a song about merry lads and lasses playing in the grass, with a hey nonny-no.

On Tuesday, the whole school day had passed like a blur for John. He was a bundle of nerves. He'd tried to stay out of Bright's way – he felt he had quite enough problems trying to remember his lines and not be sick with terror without listening to Bright moaning on about how he was going to die and nobody cared. In any case, Bright had been busy making last-minute adjustments to the lighting and video set-ups.

The final moments before the play started had seemed to go on for ever. At last, the audience had settled, the hall lights had gone out and the Elmley School production of *Julius Caesar* had begun.

John played his scenes in Act Two, and felt well-satisfied with his performance. He'd remembered all his lines, most of them in the right order. He hadn't fainted or knocked any scenery over. He was returning to the dressing room as Act Three began when he heard a noise from the props store. Curious, he stepped inside and found Bright half-heartedly tinkering with Caesar's corpse.

'Aren't you supposed to be in the lighting box?' he asked suspiciously. 'What are you doing here anyway?'

Bright sighed like a punctured airbed. 'Oh, I haven't got a cue for ages,' he said dismissively. 'I've been working on a little something special for when Mark Antony shows Caesar's body to the people of Rome,' he added in a subdued voice, 'but I don't suppose it matters now.'

John gave him a suspicious look. 'What sort of effect?'

Bright shrugged. 'I just thought it would be a terrific effect to put some lights inside the body, so that when Antony goes on about Caesar's wounds, they would all glow red as if they'd started to bleed again.'

'It sounds gross.' John had never been able to stand the sight of blood. All his sympathy for Bright disappeared as his stomach churned at the thought of it. 'You really are sick.'

'Oh, I'm sick, am I?' Bright's self-control snapped. He instantly switched to a state of furious self-pity. 'I'm going to die, and you don't care at all. All you can do is tell me I'm sick.' He reached inside the coffin and pulled out an electrical cable with a plug on the end. 'I'll show you …'

John's eyes widened. Bright had *that* look in his eyes again. Please, not another Bright disaster! He stepped forward in alarm. 'No, I didn't mean it, I'm sure it was going to be very …'

But Bright wasn't listening. 'We'll see who's sick,' he snarled. He pushed the plug into a wall socket and switched it on.

For a moment it worked. John stared into the coffin and gasped in awe as Caesar's wounds began to show as crimson gashes through his shroud.

Then a plume of smoke drifted up from the body.

John grabbed Bright's arm. 'Switch it off,' he cried.

But it was too late – even as Bright yanked the plug from its socket a tongue of flame licked up from the corpse. Squeaking in panic, John dashed into the corridor and came back with a fire extinguisher, but by this time the corpse's stuffing had melted into a smouldering sticky goo. John sprayed the remains with powder, then stared at the smoking corpse in horror.

'Look what you've done!' he moaned. 'You've ruined it!'

Bright gave a mad little laugh. 'Maybe that's how it happens,' he said, giggling. 'Maybe that's how I die! Mr Henslowe finds out what I've done and kills me!'

John shook him. 'Will you get a grip? What are we going to do? We've got to have a body! Mark Antony will be here in a minute to take it so he can show it to the crowd.'

Bright shook himself. He might be about to die, but there was a problem to be solved. Solving problems was Bright's speciality. 'We'll have to find another body,' he said.

'Terrific idea! Where are we going to find a body? They don't grow on trees, you know.' John stood for a moment in thought. Then he turned decisively to Bright. 'You'll have to do it.'

'Me?'

'It's your fault. I can't be the body, I'm supposed to be at the funeral.'

'Yes, but I'm supposed to be operating the lighting ...' Bright clicked his fingers. 'Wait a minute – the cue before Antony brings the body on is a timed fade. Once I push the button, the computer board does it all.'

John nodded. 'OK. It's got to be worth a try.' He looked up as a sound of angry shouts and a confused rushing of footsteps sounded from the stage.

'They're killing Caesar,' he told Bright. 'We haven't got long.'

Working like demons, Bright and John tipped out the smouldering remains of the corpse. John carried on clearing the coffin as Bright rushed up to the control room to set the lighting change in motion.

In the dim light, Bright reached over and punched the GO button. As he did so, his sleeve brushed the cola can he'd balanced on a shelf above the faster-than-light transmitter. The dark liquid poured into the machine.

Bright stared at it in horror. The video recording would be ruined – but there was no time to clear up the mess. Abandoning the transmitter to its fate, Bright rushed out.

After a second or two, the transmitter went *pop*!

As the Plebeians rioted on to the stage to listen

to Brutus, Bright came haring back. With a look of grim determination on his face, he eased himself into the now-empty coffin. John tucked him into his shroud, and had just covered his face when Mark Antony and the pallbearers arrived to carry the coffin onstage.

'Cor,' muttered one pallbearer as they lifted the coffin, 'this thing's got heavier since yesterday.'

'Ssh,' hissed Mark Antony.

'It's all right for you,' complained the pallbearer. 'You only have to rabbit on about what a good bloke Caesar was. You don't have to carry the great fat lump!'

Groaning and muttering, the pallbearers eased the coffin into the wings. John fell in behind.

Mr Henslowe's nerves had left him. The play was going swimmingly. Caesar had died beautifully. It was going to be all right.

Suddenly, he sat bolt upright, instantly alert as a ripple of amusement ran through the audience. Something was going wrong.

The pallbearers seemed to be having some trouble getting Caesar's corpse on to the stage. They were struggling up the steps of the forum, swaying and staggering under the weight of the coffin. Mr Henslowe was nonplussed. They hadn't had this trouble in rehearsal; the dummy Caesar was hardly any weight at all ... unless ...

Some instinct made him turn towards the lighting box.

Bright's head, with its shock of exploded hair, was nowhere to be seen. Mr Henslowe felt cold panic grip his heart as his nerves came whooping back to torment him.

Where was Bright?

'*Friends, Romans, countrymen,*' declaimed Mark Antony,

'*Lend me your ears ...*'

The pallbearers were sweating. Their muscles trembled from the strain of carrying the coffin. Their legs shook. 'Get on with it,' one of them muttered as Antony set about whipping up the Roman mob.

'Here,' cried Antony, '*under leave of Brutus and the rest,*

Come I to speak in Caesar's funeral ...'

As members of Caesar's household appeared

bearing candles and scattering flowers about their master's body, Antony signalled the pallbearers to set the coffin down. Grunting, their muscles bulging with strain, they began to lower their burden. John, standing at the head of the coffin, watched anxiously as they struggled.

Mark Antony was off again:

'He was my friend, faithful and just to me ...'

One of the pallbearers next to John gave a strangled gasp as his hand slipped.

'But Brutus says he was ambitious ...'

The coffin dropped and landed squarely on John's foot. He gave a stifled scream. From inside the coffin, a voice clearly said, 'Ow!'

Mark Antony faltered:

'And Brutus is ... er ... a horrible man ...'

John's foot throbbed. He bit his lip against the pain. His eyes filled with tears of agony.

Mark Antony recovered, and prepared to show the Plebeians the body of Caesar.

'If you have tears, prepare to shed them now.' He threw back the cloth that covered Caesar's face.

'Aaaargh!' Mark Antony stared down in shocked disbelief at the face of Vernon Bright.

Mr Henslowe whimpered and chewed the end of his tie.

'*This was the most unkindest cut of all,*' said Mark Antony in a hoarse whisper …

As the speech rumbled on Bright risked a peek about him.

There was Mark Antony, still rigid with shock and stumbling over his lines. Servants and

Plebeians stood around the coffin with heads bowed in the flickering candlelight. John stood at the head of the coffin with tears streaming down his tortured face.

Understanding flooded through Bright in a paralysing wave. Somehow, the cola spill must have set the faster-than-light transmitter working again! The picture from the show cameras was being sent four days back into the past. This was what they had seen on Saturday night! Not Bright's death, but his unplanned appearance as Caesar's corpse!

'Yehaaaah!'

Mark Antony jumped as if he had been shot and lapsed into stunned silence.

To the horror of the actors, and the mystification of the audience, the corpse of Julius Caesar leaped up.

'I'm not dead. I'm not going to die! Yahoo!'

The corpse danced around the stage, punching the air.

'It's OK,' it shrieked, 'it's OK! I'm alive!'

Mr Henslowe's eyes rolled up in his head as he slid off his chair.

*

The following Saturday morning, John went to see Bright in his lab.

After the fiasco of the opening night, Mr Henslowe had sacked Bright on the spot. Bright's grin had barely slipped. He wasn't going to die!

With Mr Henslowe operating the lights, *Julius Caesar* had completed its performance run. John had taken his last curtain call with an overwhelming sense of relief. Nobody had told him he was brilliant, but then nobody had thrown anything at him either.

Bright had recovered all his old swagger and self-esteem. As John entered the lab, he was cleaning dried cola out of the faster-than-light transmitter.

'Oh, there you are.' Bright gestured impatiently to a stool. 'I think I may have worked it out ...'

'The play went OK,' said John wearily. 'Thanks for asking.'

'What? Oh, yes ... right ... good. Anyway, the important thing is that now it's finished, I can fix the transmitter to look into the future again ...'

John gave a groan. 'Haven't you had enough of

that?' he protested. 'Don't you remember how you felt when you thought you were going to die?'

Bright shrugged. 'Well, I suppose I was a tiny bit depressed ...'

'A tiny bit!?' John threw up his hands in despair.

'... but I'm very close to finding out the secret of the faster-than-light transmitter, and from that it's but a step to the discovery of time travel ...'

A low hum echoed through the lab. A corner of the room filled with dancing blue sparks. The air tasted of tin.

With a *pop*, a second Vernon Bright materialized out of thin air. He glared at John and Bright, who were staring at him open-mouthed.

'Don't even think about it,' said Bright Two.

John managed to get his mouth working. 'Whu? Wha? Huh?'

'Time travel,' said Bright Two. 'It's bad news. Take it from me.'

Bright found his voice at last. 'But you're me,' he stammered.

'Exactly,' snapped Bright Two, 'so I know what I'm talking about.'

There was another atmospheric disturbance and another *pop*.

'Don't listen to him,' said Bright Three as he materialized. He turned to Bright Two. 'If he doesn't invent a time machine, you won't exist.'

Bright Two glared at Bright Three. 'So how come *you* exist?'

Hum – sparkle – *pop*.

'Don't answer that,' commanded Bright Four. 'The paradoxes are enough to make your brain explode ...'

John sat in a daze watching Bright arguing with three copies of himself. He sighed. It looked as though Bright would never learn. He'd probably go on making the same mistakes over and over again.

Time ... after time ... after ...